It started far off . . .

somewhere at the other end of another universe. Resembling fragments of quivering crimson jelly, they rushed at him. Then they grew in size until they were huge, blood-red balloons.

Then they hit his brain, and the backs of his eyes burst into tiny pieces, each hammering every nerve ending in his body.

So this is it, Carter thought. *At last I've found out what it's like to be dead. . . .*

NICK CARTER IS IT!

FROM THE NICK CARTER
KILLMASTER SERIES

NICK CARTER

KILLMASTER

The Normandy Code

CHARTER BOOKS, NEW YORK

THE NORMANDY CODE

A Charter Book/published by arrangement with
The Condé Nast Publications, Inc.

PRINTING HISTORY
Charter Original/July 1985

ISBN: 0-441-58612-0

Charter Books are published by The Berkley Publishing Group,
200 Madison Avenue, New York, New York 10016.
PRINTED IN THE UNITED STATES OF AMERICA

Dedicated to the men of the
Secret Services of the
United States of America

The Normandy Code

ONE

Norman Ahrens had been with the government in one way or another for twenty-five of his fifty years. The last three had been spent as West Berlin Operations Manager for Kennecut Paper Products.

It was a small firm with a low volume of business. It was kept that way so it didn't take too much time away from Ahrens's real job of running agents back and forth through the wall for the CIA.

When his secretary buzzed him with what she termed a "strange and evidently urgent" call, Ahrens was about to wrap up the day's work and spend the afternoon playing handball at the American Club.

"Yes?"

"Norman Ahrens?"

"Yes." The voice was low and sultry, the English spoken with just the hint of an accent he couldn't place. "Who is this?"

"Is this phone clean?"

"I don't know what you mean," he lied.

"I think you do, Mr. Ahrens. Kennecut Paper is a front for your real work . . . that work is acting as control for several West German agents operating in the East."

"The phone is clean."

1

"Good. My name is Tamara Petrovna Rogozina. I am a KGB agent currently on assignment in West Berlin."

Ahrens's forehead broke out in a cool sweat. "So?"

"I won't be in your files. I have only been active for two years since my training."

"Why do you tell me all this?"

"Because, Norman Ahrens, *you* are in *our* files. This is Friday. Tomorrow afternoon at four o'clock there will be a funeral in Wasselheim. It is a small village not far from Wolfsburg, on the Western side of the border. Do you know it?"

"I know it. A friend of yours?"

"The deceased's name is Horst Buckner. He is the son of the village baker. He was killed in a motorcar accident. I got his name from the newspaper obituary column. I must talk to you. Will you attend that funeral?"

"How do I know you are who you say you are?"

There was a short pause, and then the voice came back on the line, slightly more strident.

"For the last three years you have run a double agent. Here in Germany his name was Hans Gebbler. In Russia he was known as Georgi Yushenkov."

The perspiration was even colder now, and it covered his whole body. He said nothing. Georgi Yushenkov was a money-grubbing, woman-chasing asshole, but he supplied a lot of information.

"You'll find Gebbler/Yushenkov in his apartment. He is dead. I severed his spine with a stiletto two hours ago while he was making love to me."

As Norman Ahrens settled into the front seat of the rented car, he cursed the woman, cursed his own foolishness, and cursed the weather.

For the last hour and ten minutes he had stood, hatless in the rain, listening to a priest pray over the last remains of a German baker's son and watching the family weep.

At the cemetery gate he paused to check traffic in the creeping fog.

"Hey, man, how about a lift into town?"

She sounded American and looked like a teen-ager, complete with the uniform: jeans and sneakers, T-shirt emblazoned with NO NUKES, and a tennis sweatband around her forehead holding her long dark hair.

Ahrens shook his head.

"Hey, c'mon, man, give a girl a break. I'm soaked to my skin!"

"Can't do it. Sorry, but I've got to meet someone."

"Huh? . . . Can't hear you. . ."

Ahrens leaned across and rolled the window down about four inches. "I said. . ."

The rest of the words got choked in his throat. The snout of a 9mm Beretta was pointed directly between his eyes.

"Unlock the door, Mr. Ahrens."

They were parked in a narrow lane under a grove of trees. It was pitch dark now, and the rain still beat down in blinding sheets.

The handkerchief in Norman Ahrens's hand was soaked with perspiration from constantly mopping his brow.

"So that's it."

And that's quite a story, he thought. This woman, for there was little doubt in his mind now that she was far from a teen-ager, had just related the complete rundown of her training as a KGB agent. She had also given him the names of three American businessmen who had been subverted in the last year.

"So you want to defect."

"I do."

"When?"

"Not now," she said, turning her eyes to his. "But soon, I hope."

"Why?"

"I know, from my training and from what I have seen here in West Berlin, that one must have money to survive in the West. As much as they deny it, it is the same in the Soviet Union."

"So you want money."

"I am willing to trade something for enough money to start a new life and a new identity."

"What do you have to trade?"

Again those eyes burrowed into his, shaking the equilibrium of a man who had been in the business for years. He thought of the previous evening, of Yushenkov's skinny, lifeless, nude body on the bed. There had been only a few drops of blood: a very professional hit.

And the beautiful creature who was now sitting alongside him had done it, done it while he was making love to her.

Ahrens shivered. He had never killed a man. He was a manipulator, not a killer, and when he came up against one, especially a good one, a pro, he always found himself in awe.

"Your computer security at NATO headquarters in Brussels has been breached."

"Impossible."

"Only a complacent American would say that, Mr. Ahrens. Believe me, it has been done."

"By whom?"

"That I do not know, but I will in two weeks' time."

Bells clanged in Ahrens's brain. Not bells of alarm, but of anticipation. In an instant, his mood changed to resemble the wolf who has caught the scent of fresh meat. "Explain."

She did, in a quiet, evenly modulated voice. "In two weeks' time a man will arrive in Paris. I am to be his contact. I am to supply him with new papers and clear the way for him to board an Aeroflot flight to Moscow."

"And you don't know his identity?"

"I know him only by the code name 'Madonna,' and that is the extent of my information. I am to procure customs clearance for an ivory Madonna that is supposedly a relic of the Russian Orthodox Church stolen during the war. My guess is that the Madonna contains whatever secrets the man has obtained.''

No sweat now, only calm deliberation. This kind of horse trading Norman Ahrens understood.

Jesus Christ, he thought, *what a coup.*

"If what you say is true, I don't think there is any doubt that my government will meet any price you ask.''

"I want one thing understood, even if it is just between you and me.''

"Go on.''

"I am not a moral person. Indeed, they have made me amoral. It is their way. I have killed, and may well have to kill again. I have done many other things that would be abhorrent to any . . . any normal person. When I say I want money, it is only for a new life. I do not desire riches, only security . . . so I never have to do these things again. I am now a subhuman, a coldly calculating machine. One day I want to feel like a human being, and a woman, again.''

"I think I understand.''

Ahrens took a pad from his inside coat pocket and jotted a number down. He tore the sheet away and handed it to her.

"Contact this number in Paris. Identify yourself as . . . uh, Diana.''

She glanced at the paper, blinked once, and tore it into tiny pieces. Ahrens only nodded. He knew that the number was already indelibly inscribed on her brain.

Indeed, he thought, *she is trained as she claims.*

"It is the number of your people in Paris?''

"No, another agency,'' Ahrens replied. "One that is more adept at this sort of operation.''

"What agency?''

"I don't know. Like your people, mine have certain men for certain jobs. I would guess that extreme measures may have to be taken with this 'Madonna' person. The people I am sending you to are equipped to take those measures.''

Ahrens knew by the brief cloud that passed over her eyes that further explanation was unnecessary.

If terminating "Madonna" was necessary, the certain men Ahrens referred to were totally capable of that termination.

Ahrens continued. "If we recover this Madonna, I will arrange funds for you in a Swiss bank, and papers for a new life under a new identity."

"And if the statue, for some reason, is not recovered . . . ?"

"Then, my dear, you will probably be thrown to the wolves . . . your own people. I'm sure you understand?"

"I do," she replied without a quiver in her voice. She reached for the door handle. "Good-bye, Norman Ahrens. I will keep my part of the bargain. See that you keep yours."

With that, she slipped from the car and disappeared in the gathering fog.

Ahrens shivered. He suddenly felt an odd, cold chill from the seat she had just vacated.

With a slightly quivering hand, he engaged the car's gear box and headed back to West Berlin.

Two hours later, he was on a scrambler phone to his superiors at Langley. At the conclusion of his call, an emergency meeting was called.

The results of the meeting were in unanimous agreement with Norman Ahrens's first thought.

David Hawk, head of AXE, was contacted and briefed on the Madonna affair.

Less than five hours after Tamara Petrovna Rogozina had left Norman Ahrens's car in Germany, Nick Carter, AXE agent N3, the Killmaster, was summoned to the AXE offices on Dupont Circle.

TWO

Julian Carmont moved his tall, lithe body like an eel through the gamblers occupying the main room of the Deauville casino. Compared to other men in the sedate room, he was dressed casually in an off-white silk shirt, a wine-colored tie, and a medium gray lightweight suit.

He perused the blackjack tables, the chemin-de-fer table, and then moved on. At the third roulette table, Carmont's cool eyes found the face he sought among the bored croupiers.

The table was full. Carmont waited, idly riffling two-hundred-franc chips in his long-fingered, powerful hands. Finally an overweight, overly made-up matron slapped the table in disgust and stood. A young man, blond, very pretty, and barely a third her age, consolingly slipped his arm around her thick waist.

"Come, *ma chérie*, to the bar. A drink or two and you will relax . . . play better."

"I've lost twenty thousand."

"So? What is twenty thousand to you, *ma petite*? Now, about my new car. . ."

Carmont let a smile stretch his thin lips beneath a dark

7

mustache, and he slid into the vacated seat. He fingered a five-thousand-franc chip from his vest pocket and whirled it expertly across the felt toward the croupier at the end.

"Changez, s'il vous plaît."

The croupier glanced up and quickly back down to the rack of chips at his elbow. He had barely blinked his recognition at Julian Carmont, but it was enough. They were old friends, not in public, but in the shadowy underworld of France from Paris to Marseille to Dieppe.

The croupier's name was Pierre Donet, and in league with Carmont he had stolen hundreds of thousands of marks, pounds, francs, and dollars all over Europe.

But never in Normandy. Normandy was home. In Normandy they were respected, hard-working men: Donet a croupier, Carmont the owner of a stylish boutique on the fashionable rue Gontaut-Biron.

With his stick, Donet pushed even piles of chips back to Carmont. He then barely turned his head to the master croupier sitting on a high stool behind.

"Une pause, monsieur, s'il vous plaît?"

"Oui." The master nodded.

Donet rose from the table, stretched, and moved away to take his bihourly break. Carmont had timed his entrance perfectly. Another tuxedoed croupier took Donet's place, and Carmont scattered chips across the numbers at random.

The wheel spun, the ball rolled and dropped.

He had no winner, and repeated his random bets.

Again the action, again no winner.

With a shrug, Carmont placed his remaining thousand francs on number 25. It was the next day's date.

The ball rolled lazily in its groove, dropped, tinkled over three numbers, and came to rest in the slot of number 25.

He collected thirty thousand in five-thousand-franc chips, and sailed the odd one-thousand-franc chip across to the croupier as a tip.

"Merci, monsieur."

Carmont nonchalantly pocketed his winnings and moved from the room. He strode down the wide, chandeliered outer hall and into the banquet room.

A boule table had been set up to accommodate those who wanted to gamble but did not desire the higher stakes of the main room.

A pair of pretty girls at the end of the table smiled and greeted him. Carmont blew them a kiss and moved on without pausing for conversation.

They were both shopgirls employed in his boutique. On his return to the main room he would stop for idle chatter, but now he was intent.

Pierre Donet had only a twenty-minute break.

On the lower level, he moved with greater purpose through the twin doors of the w.c. Inside, he pushed open the door marked *Hommes,* and paused.

Donet was at the sinks, washing his hands. Their eyes caught briefly in the mirror, and the croupier inclined his head once toward the rear stall and held up one finger.

Carmont moved across the gaudily tiled floor and stopped at a sink beside the other man. He twisted both faucets on until the rushing water would blur their whispered voices.

Donet spoke first, his words a bare mumble between hardly moving lips.

"Did you win?"

"Quite a bit. I played twenty-five."

Donet chuckled. "A good omen. Are we on?"

"We are. I'm driving to Paris yet tonight."

"The hardware?"

"Carmine and Alain have it all. They left this morning in the van."

"And Dino Foche?" Donet asked, his hard eyes in the mirror darkening.

"Still sober and being watched by Claudia like a hawk. Marta should be giving them a final briefing right now." Carmont paused, studying the darkening cloud that had appeared in his friend's face. "You still don't approve of Dino."

"No, I do not. A drunk is a drunk, and too dangerous in a job of this size."

Carmont shrugged. "He's the best drill man in France, and the only man who can handle a Selston laser without burning up the goods."

"Perhaps," Donet replied, tight-lipped. "Let us hope Claudia's sex will substitute for the alcohol long enough."

Carmont smiled. "She is your mistress, my friend. You should know her capabilities. Your people on the outside?"

"Taken care of. The garbage men are bought and paid for, and the truck driver knows where to pick up and deliver in Honfleur."

"Excellent," Carmont nodded, drying his hands. "Until Paris."

"Until Paris."

High above Deauville, on Mount Conisy, lay the rambling Hôtel du Golf. From her fourth floor rear suite, Marta Penn sipped a Campari and Perrier and watched the moonlight stream in iridescent waves over the sloping fairways and manicured greens of the golf course.

Outwardly, her high-cheekboned, fine-featured face was calm. But beneath the serene beauty she was a mass of fear and trembling nerves.

Could they do it? Would they be caught? And if they were, could Marta Penn, pampered socialite and ex-high fashion model, survive years of punishment in a filthy French prison?

It had all started four years before, in Marbella, Spain. She had gone on vacation to bake on the Spanish beaches and try to put the pieces of her life back together.

It had been difficult.

In her teens, Marta had inherited vast wealth and, at the same time, solidified a career as a top fashion model in the U.K. and on the Continent.

She had been too young to realize that the ride she was on could ever have an ending.

But it did.

For fifteen years, she lived on the edge and at the top. Then one morning she woke up, broke and thirty-four years old. The photographers no longer needed her services, and her dressmaker would no longer accept her orders for new clothes until the last year's bills were paid.

Marta took the last of her money and headed for Marbella. In the back of her mind, she hoped to meet a wealthy dowager.

Instead she met Julian Carmont, on the surface a monied, genteel adventurer descended from French landed gentry.

For six months it was the old life again. And then Julian's money ran out, and Marta quickly learned about the real Julian.

They were in Nice.

"You can do it, Marta. I know what kind of woman you can be in bed," Julian had whispered huskily, turning on the full wattage of his considerable charm. "He holds the key to it all. The casino is prime. With the floor plan and the key to unlock the security system, we can buy ourselves another year on the Riviera."

Marta couldn't resist, either the thrill of danger or the promise of money.

His name was Carlos Raphael, and Marta seduced him three hours after their first meeting.

In a week's time, she had the information Julian needed. In three weeks' time, they robbed the Nice casino of just over 15 million francs.

But Carlos Raphael was smart. He put two and two together, and came up with Marta.

She was surprised when the showdown came. She had been able to kill Raphael without batting an eye.

"Excellent, Marta, excellent," Julian had said. "You have no fear. That is important in our business!"

That was only the beginning. In the last four years, they had pulled three more large-scale robberies, and twice more Marta had been forced to kill in cold blood.

Even Julian now respected and feared her.

"I think you are now my peer, Marta. One day, perhaps, you will even surpass me. We both must be very careful."

Now they were about to pull the most dangerous job ever. Marta didn't fear the risks of the job. She looked forward to them.

What she did fear was Julian Carmont's waning interest in her as a mistress. Somehow, in the depths of her mind, she knew that once the job was done, Julian Carmont was going to kill her.

The phone jangled in the suite behind her, jarring her already frayed nerves so that a goodly amount of the red liquid in her glass splashed across the polished tile of the terrace.

"Damn!"

She was sure it was Julian. He would want her report on Claudia and Dino. What could she tell him? She hadn't seen the whore or the drunk since lunch.

"Yes?"

"Marta, it's Claudia . . ."

"Where the hell have you been?"

"Marta, I couldn't help it. We were in the sauna. He said he was just going to the men's . . ."

The rest of the girl's words were choked off by whining sobs.

"He got a bottle."

"Yes. I found him in a cave down on the beach about an hour ago."

"Where are you now?"

"In our suite. I—"

"Never mind. Stay there, and keep Dino there. I'll be right down!"

Marta slammed the phone down and flew from the suite

without bothering to change out of the flowing green robe she was wearing. It fanned out behind her like a cape as she ran through the wide corridors and fire doors to the opposite wing of the huge, rambling hotel.

"Yes?" came the little-girl voice in answer to Marta's frantic rapping.

"It's me! Open the door!"

The door was flung aside, and Marta was faced with a distraught, almost hysterical Claudia Biget. The skintight white jump suit she wore was wet and filthy. The zipper was broken, allowing the two sides of the suit to gap open, revealing twin mountains of creamy flesh.

She was young, in her early twenties, but her Kewpie-doll face already had that brittle, used look so common to young girls who had seen twice the life of their years. Her usually well-coiffed blond hair was soaked with perspiration and plastered to her forehead. Twin rivers of mascara streaked down her cheeks.

Marta had barely closed the door behind her when the other woman launched into a sobbing, arm-waving explanation, all in French.

"English," Marta hissed, "speak in English!"

Still French, and so fast that Marta could barely understand a single word. She repeated the command, and accompanied it with a violent shaking of Claudia's shoulders.

When that did no good, she hit the girl, full on the left cheek with her right palm. The sharp sound of flesh on flesh was like the crack of a rifle in the room, and was quickly followed by a backhand that twisted Claudia's head far around over her left shoulder.

A last resounding whack spun her across the room to tumble over a chair and flop unceremoniously on her wide derrière.

This time, when she stared up at the she-demon with the smoldering green eyes and the clenched fists hovering over her, Claudia spoke in English.

"He must have planned it. He took my clothes from outside the sauna. I forgot and left money in my purse. He probably used that to buy the bottles . . ."

"Bottles? My God . . ."

"There were two. By the time I stole this jump suit from a locker and found him, he was halfway through the second one."

"Damn," Marta spat. "How did you get him back up here?"

"The service elevator. There wasn't a scene, Marta—no one saw us, I swear!"

"Let us hope so. Where is he?"

"In the shower."

Marta whirled, her sharp heels clicking on the polished hardwood floor. "Order some coffee from room service, and tell them to hurry!"

Dino Foche lay half in, half out of the tub, his wrinkled, aging body shivering beneath the blast of cold water from the shower.

Marta curled her fingers in the fringe of gray hair behind his bald pate and turned his face full into the blast.

She stared down at the naked American's walruslike body and the heavily veined, red-splotched face with contempt. There were large pouches of baggy skin under the eyes, and when the eyes themselves blinked open, the whites looked like road maps.

"Lemme alone, lemme be." The voice was a rasp and the flailing arms were ineffectual.

"You're a stinking lush, Dino, but you're all we've got," Marta hissed. "Because of that, I'll smooth this over with Julian. But if this happens again I'll tell him everything. And you know what Julian will do, Dino."

"Screw you and screw Julian. Gimme a drink and I'll be fine."

"No booze, Dino . . . coffee."

As if on cue, Claudia entered the bathroom with a tray. She

had combed her hair and managed to pin the jump suit together.

"Pour him a cup . . . black."

Claudia did, then held it to the old man's lips.

"I don't want that crap!" he growled. "I hate the stuff and it's cold anyway!"

"Drink it, Dino," Marta ordered, shoving his head forward.

He took a large gulp and promptly spit it into Claudia's face.

Marta's reaction was abrupt and instant. She shoved his head underwater and held him there. When she was sure his lungs were about to burst, she pulled him up for a short breath, and then dunked him again.

"Marta, *mon Dieu*, you'll kill him!" Claudia cried.

"Do you care?"

Claudia dropped her eyes from the other woman's cold stare. She hated Dino and the fact that she had been elected his babysitter, but she didn't want to see him die . . . especially since they were registered as husband and wife in the hotel.

Claudia was constantly afraid of the consequences of what she was, a whore used by everybody.

But she was even more afraid of Marta. Underneath the tall model's beautiful, cultured exterior, Claudia sensed reality: Marta was a killer.

"Get out," Marta snapped, hauling the sputtering, gasping Dino up from the water and out over the side of the tub.

Claudia literally flew from the room, closing the door behind her. Marta poured another cup of coffee and carefully set it beside Dino's quivering hand. She then stood and searched in a leather shaving kit by the tub.

From a pack of twelve, she extracted one single-edged blade and turned to stare down at Dino Foche.

"You're a pig, Dino. You look like a bloated, beached whale."

"Screw you."

"Drink the coffee, Dino."

"Put some good American bourbon in it first."

She moved so quickly that even if Dino had had his faculties about him he couldn't have stopped her. In one swift movement, Marta gathered his genitals in her left hand and held the gleaming razor blade between the thumb and forefinger of her right hand, directly over his eyes.

"You'll drink the coffee, Dino, and you'll sober up. And once you're sober, you'll stay that way until the job is done."

"You wouldn't."

"Yes, I would, Dino. Oh, you'll bleed a lot, but you'll live. Drink, Dino, or go through the rest of your miserable life a eunuch."

"You're a cold bitch."

"Yes, I am."

She lowered the blade to his belly and barely creased the skin, just enough to draw a red line, perfectly straight, clear to his crotch.

"Jesus Christ . . ."

"Drink, Dino."

He did, in great gulps, and when the cup was empty, he poured it full again himself.

"Good, Dino, very good."

Marta found Claudia coiled like a taut spring on the sitting room sofa.

"He's drinking the coffee, and I have his word that he'll stay sober."

"How did you do that?"

"I threatened to cut off what manhood he has left with a razor blade."

Claudia's stark white face went gray, and her lungs couldn't seem to get any air. For a moment, Marta was sure the girl would faint. When she didn't, Marta continued.

"It will be up to you to make sure he keeps his word."

"*Mon Dieu*, how can I . . . ?"

"You will, that's all," Marta cooed, leaning down until her nose almost touched Claudia's. "Because if you don't, little girl, I'll kill you. Just as sure as there are fish in the sea, I'll take my little pearl-handled gun and put a bullet right between those big, dumb, vacant eyes of yours."

Julian was in the suite when Marta returned. He was pacing and smoking, but other than that, and a slight vee in his heavy black brows, there was no sign of anger or frustration.

But Marta knew him. She knew the little signs. Inside, he was boiling.

"I told you not to leave the room."

"I had to go over to Dino and Claudia's suite."

"An emergency?"

"No, not really."

"*Merde.* You run around hotel halls in your robe . . ." Abruptly he reached out and tugged the satin sash at her waist. The robe above and below bloused open. "And nothing else?"

"All right. Dino slipped away from Claudia. He had a few drinks."

"A few? How few?"

"A few. It's all right. I can handle it."

"Can you?"

"Yes, dammit, I can! Give me a cigarette."

He shook one from a pack and smiled when he saw the tremble in her fingers as she reached for it.

Marta also saw the tremble, and hated herself for it. Julian Carmont was the only man alive who could make her tremble.

"We're on, Marta. It's go for tomorrow night. Pierre has his end ready. We need Dino, and we need him sober."

"He'll be there, and he'll be sober."

In the fleeting instant Marta saw his face before bending over the lighter he held, she felt as though she were looking at a stranger, not anyone she had ever seen before, let alone slept with for almost five years.

As smoke curled from the cigarette, she slowly raised her head until their eyes met.

She hadn't tightened the belt back around her waist after he had pulled it. Now she could see Julian's eyes invading the shadows under the partially opened robe.

"When are you leaving for Paris?" she asked, her voice low, husky.

"Now. I'll take the Jaguar. You and the others come down in the morning in the Mercedes."

"It's only a two-hour drive on the *péage*. You can spare a half hour, Julian . . ."

With the cigarette curling smoke from the corner of her mouth, Marta shrugged the robe from her shoulders. Languidly, she removed the cigarette from her lips and dropped it into an ashtray.

As she moved toward him she detected the flash of naked lust that always entered his eyes each time he saw her nude.

European photographers may have stopped wanting Marta Penn's face, but no man she had ever known had stopped wanting her body.

She was tall, with small, darkly nippled breasts, and a perfect female line of form down across her waist, hips, and thighs.

She moved into his arms with her face upturned and her lips open in a sensuous pout.

"We'll win, Julian. By the day after tomorrow, we'll be rich . . . again."

"We always win, Marta."

As he kissed her, Marta felt a mounting excitement surging deep inside her. But she knew that only part of it was due to Julian. He always affected her physically; she had never denied that.

But deep down, Marta knew that it wasn't Julian or the sex he offered that was exciting her.

It was the job, and the danger it would bring. The thrill of danger to her was more satisfying than physical sex could ever be.

Tomorrow night they would rip off an entire hotel, the richest, poshest hotel in Paris.

Tomorrow night, they would rape the Ritz.

THREE

The Brussels to Paris express was just under an hour late pulling out. But it mattered little to the gray-haired man with the darting blue eyes and the wrinkled features that had sported a beatific smile since he had first slid into the seat.

When the train gently rolled forward, he leaned back and lit an American cigarette. He made a mental note to purchase as many cartons of the brand as possible before boarding the plane to Moscow two days hence.

Working with the Americans, as he had for the last four years, had spoiled him in many ways. He had grown fond of a certain brand of whiskey made in a place called Tennessee, as well as the cigarettes.

These things would be impossible to acquire in Moscow. But giving them up would be only a slight inconvenience compared to the rewards he would reap as a hero of the Soviet Union.

This thought widened the smile on his face. He drew deeply from the cigarette in his right hand, and let the fingers of his left play across the attaché case on his lap.

The case contained his passport, two changes of underwear, a fresh shirt, and some socks. Carefully cushioned among these articles was his life savings in Deutsche marks and French francs, and an eight-inch-by-six-inch leather case.

The case was lined in velvet, and resting securely in its velvet niche was the Madonna. It was made from bone-white ivory, and had been crafted to exact specifications by a Belgian artisan named Johan Pheffer.

Within an hour after its delivery, Johan Pheffer was dead, his body deposited in a long-abandoned well on the outskirts of Brussels.

Pheffer would have been killed even if he had not been curious about the strange construction of the Madonna. There could be no loose ends, no curious questions that could be answered by a man who knew the answers without knowing that he knew.

And Pheffer had begun to suspect, even before he was half finished with the elaborate, highly detailed design.

Etched into the Babe's swaddling clothes and into the skirt of the Virgin, as well as her crown, were the exact sites of every missile in Europe and England, as well as the computer codes that would render those missiles useless.

It had taken Almar Koenigburger three years to get this information. Tiny bit by tiny bit he had painstakingly extracted it from the master computers at NATO Command in Brussels and woven it into the design of the Madonna.

"But with such detail, Herr Koenigburger, I will have time for nothing else! The cost—"

"Cost, Herr Pheffer, is of no importance. The clergy that I represent expect to pay."

Pheffer began to suspect that there was no clergy, but his pay was so great and so prompt that he kept his curiosity to a minimum.

Until the final mold.

"It is odd, Herr Koenigburger, this design. Part of it seems to be numbers, some kind of formula. And here, in the planes of the skirt . . . it appears to be a map . . ."

With those words Johan Pheffer had definitely sealed his fate and signed his own death warrant.

Koenigburger mashed out his cigarette, stood, and, still, clutching the attaché case, opened the door of the compartment. He walked toward the end of the car and the toilets with a decided limp in his left leg.

The limp was a result of a wound from a Russian rifle during the Red Army's final surge through Berlin during the closing days of the war.

It was ironic that the youth, Almar Koenigburger, had been wounded with a Russian bullet. Prior to the war he had been in the forefront of the Communist youth party in Berlin. Not openly, of course. Openly, he was a good son of the Fatherland, a rapt disciple of Herr Hitler. And, as such, he was able to worm his way into a position as a cipher clerk in the Reichstag.

As a result of this position, he had passed secret after secret to the advancing Russian army.

Later, during the occupation, he was sent to a refugee-detention-concentration camp in the Ukraine.

At least that was what his records in Allied Intelligence had shown.

In actual fact, Almar Koenigburger had been sent to school in the village of Sveldenstag, outside Moscow. There he was further indoctrinated with Communist ideology, and trained intensively as a spy and a mole. All this was done for the day when he could perform his one great act of espionage for the Communist cause.

Eventually he was repatriated and gained employment with the newly formed West German government in Bonn. He worked hard, and developed a brilliant ability as a systems analyst and went on to become a computer programmer. Through clever maneuvering, he procured an assignment to NATO Command in Brussels as part of the West German contingent.

Over the years, Koenigburger had meticulously lifted codes, key phrases, and interdicts from various other programmers and stored them away as a desert pack rat stores shiny baubles.

Because of this, it was easy for Almar to finally become active when word came from his Amsterdam control.

At the age of sixty-one, Almar Koenigburger was given his one great task as an espionage agent: obtain the number of missiles in Western Europe and England, their exact location, their precise range, and the method of activation as well as their fail-safe codes.

The years of groundwork made the assignment child's play for Koenigburger.

Three weeks before, he had made the drop in Brussels: *Have completed Madonna. Await coming out procedures.*

Two days later, he retrieved his instructions from the same drop: *You are code-named Madonna. On 25 this month train to Paris. Contact to be made with female agent code-named Raven. Drop Ritz Hotel reserved in your name.*

Koenigburger emerged from the w.c. with yet a new glint in his eyes. He would have two last days in Paris, and he meant to enjoy them to the fullest. He would drink good French cognac, visit the Lido, and end his evening by splurging his Western money on a beautiful woman. Maybe even two beautiful women.

He returned to his seat and lovingly cradled the attaché case on his lap. He napped, only to be awakened by a child of four with drooling jowls, wet breeches, and the lungs of an opera singer trying to crawl into his lap.

The child was barely saved from a concussion by a seemingly complacent mother with two other brats and an ugly Pekingese-looking mongrel in tow.

"*Pardon, monsieur, pardon,*" the woman said, tugging the screeching child away.

"*Madame?*"

"*Oui?*"

"*Parlez-vous anglais?*"

"*Non, monsieur,*" she replied with a shake of her head.

"Good," Koenigburger said icily, lapsing into English. "At the very least, your little monster should be institutionalized until he is an adult. At the most, he should be drawn, quartered, parboiled, and freeze-dried, as food for the underprivileged masses of the world."

Almar Koenigburger had little time for people in general, but he particularly detested prepubescent children.

The woman didn't understand a word he said, but the ominous gleam in his eyes and the harsh tone in his voice told her that she, her dog, and her brood were not wanted.

Without another word, she moved to another compartment, leaving the vile-smelling little man to his thoughts of glory and the attaché case he protected with so much vigor.

This was precisely as the squatly built German wanted it. He napped at ease the remainder of the way into Paris, and emerged from the train refreshed and ready for his night of debauchery.

"Monsieur?" the cabdriver asked, flipping the meter before his passenger had settled into the seat.

"Le Ritz, si'l vous plaît," Koenigburger replied.

"Oui, monsieur."

As the taxi approached the hotel, Koenigburger's eyes grew wide and his pulse quickened. He was impressed. The Ritz fronted on the Place Vendôme, with its exclusive shops and milling, beautiful people. It gladdened his pumping heart so much that he overtipped the driver, and even tipped the doorman though he had no luggage to wrestle.

"Lost," he shrugged in response to the questioning look. "You know the airlines."

"Oui, monsieur. I am sorry" came the knowing reply. "If you will inform the concierge, it will be taken to your room upon its immediate arrival."

"Merci."

He was amazed at how small the reception area was: a narrow foyer, an unimpressive desk, and only one clerk.

"You have a reservation, *monsieur?*"

"Oui. Koenigburger, Almar Koenigburger."

"Of course. May I see your passport, please?"

It was produced, and the young clerk immediately shifted into fluent German.

"Your room is ready, *mein Herr.* Can we be of any further service at this time?"

"Yes, as a matter of fact, you can," Koenigburger replied, opening his attaché case and glancing to his left, where a door was open to a long bank of safe-deposit boxes. "I would like to put this in safekeeping."

"Of course, *mein Herr*."

Koenigburger hesitated for an instant. "Your safe-deposit boxes . . . they are safe?"

"*Mein Herr*, this *is* the Ritz."

FOUR

The tall, wide-shouldered American with the sharply chiseled features and the heavy-lidded dark eyes sat with his back to the wall, surveying his fellow drinkers in the upstairs lounge of Orly Airport.

A half-finished aperitif and an open menu rested on the immaculate white linen tablecloth near his right hand. He had no intention of dining, and the drink had been ordered only to keep the table, a place to sit and wait.

Even if he had been hungry, he knew he couldn't eat. His stomach was in knots.

It smelled, all of it.

The defecting Russian agent, Tamara Petrovna Rogozina, had thus far not told them any lies. But that meant very little to Nick Carter. The Killmaster knew from years of experience that the KGB could set you up with fifty small truths and then spring the big lie.

And it was the big lie that got you killed.

He had arrived in France via London, Dover, and Calais nine days before, after a full briefing from chief of AXE operations, David Hawk. The "full" briefing was actually only a nibble of information and a lot of speculation.

"We'll set up a pre-meet outside Paris, through the Paris office. The judgment is yours, N3. If you think it's a go, we go. If not . . ."

"If not, terminate her and get out."

"Right, but not before you're sure. If Madonna is for real, the info he has could be a time bomb. Changing missile locations could cost billions, not to mention the time and money that would be expended in creating new launch and fail-safe codes."

"And we have nothing on the woman, Rogozina?"

"Absolutely nothing beyond Norman Ahrens's description and what she herself has volunteered."

"If she's been active for only two years, that would be understandable."

"It would," Hawk had said, frowning through the habitual cloud of cigar smoke hovering around his head. "But it would be just like the KGB to set her up for us so this Madonna could slip through with no info. But we couldn't take the chance."

"And we revise NATO missiles for nothing."

"Right. It would be right up their alley."

Norman Ahrens had set up the meet in the ancient city of Reims. The location was perfect for the woman coming from Germany and Carter driving down from Calais. It was an hour and a half by train, and almost the same by car on into Paris, once Carter had assured himself that the defecting Russian woman was the genuine article.

If the Killmaster's reaction was negative, there were fields upon fields of champagne vineyards where a body would not be discovered for years.

Ahrens had wisely chosen the Hôtel La Paix. It was in the very center of the city's activity, with the streets around it filled with summer tourists. Adding to its anonymity were the more than one hundred rooms and its almost daily transient, mostly tourist, clientele.

Carter checked in at six o'clock sharp, ordered a bottle of the best local bubbly, and sat down to wait.

The knock came at two minutes past midnight. The time brought a smile to Carter's face. He had already checked the train schedules. The through train from Mannheim to Paris stopped in Reims at 11:45 for a one-hour layover.

Tamara Rogozina was sharp. If she didn't like the situation and decided to rid herself of the contact Ahrens had set up—namely, Nick Carter—she had a getaway ready and waiting.

Carter blinked when he opened the door and saw what was on the threshold. She was blonde, wearing an ice-blue sheath that gleamed with expense. Her throat and arms were nearly as white as her gloves and bag.

"Monsieur Rolland?" she asked, her eyes appraising him with one long, cool look.

"Yes."

She extended a gloved hand, and Carter took from it one half of a hundred-mark note. It matched the other half in his own hand.

But even with the match, Carter's forehead furrowed. She saw it, and a faint smile touched a corner of her overly red mouth. She inclined her sleek, golden head ever so slightly toward the room.

"I think I can explain better inside."

"Of course."

Carter stepped aside, moving his right shoulder and arm behind the door. A tensing of his forearm muscle freed his pencil-thin stiletto, Hugo, from its chamois sheath and into his palm.

If this were indeed Tamara Petrovna Rogozina, she looked nothing like the description Norman Ahrens had given.

She moved by him with a delicate gracefulness, her eyes hitting every corner of the single room.

Carter closed the door and dropped his arm, hiding Hugo behind his right thigh.

"The room is clean?" she said, peeling the gloves from her hands.

"I'm sure the maids have made sure it is. The La Paix is a good hotel."

"That's not what I mean," she said, whirling, her voice dropping a full octave and letting a slight accent creep into her English.

"It isn't?"

Then she understood, and smiled. Carter found it quite a nice smile, but he didn't relax.

"It is the way I look."

"It could be."

"The blond hair is a wig. I'm afraid the voluptuousness of my figure is also false. I am actually quite small and my figure very petite. As for the expensive clothes, it is often good to become inconspicuous by being looked at."

Carter relaxed, even smiled. "You don't look like a gangly little teen-ager. Champagne?"

"Please, thank you."

She moved to the sofa. Carter slid Hugo back home, then poured two glasses. He handed her one and took the chair opposite.

"You have less than an hour to reboard your train," he said, shaking a cigarette from the pack on the table between them. "Perhaps you should begin."

"Excellent," she chuckled, genuinely. "You guessed my timing."

Carter nodded. "It wouldn't have done you any good, but it was an intelligent move."

She shook her head as he offered the cigarettes. "Are you positive now that my request is genuine and I am what I say?"

"No."

"But you're not sure that I am a fake, either."

"No. That's why you're still alive."

Again she chuckled. "Are you so sure you can kill me?"

"Yes. Quite sure."

"I believe you," she replied matter-of-factly, her points going up with Carter when she could admit it and still keep the amusement in her eyes. "What is your real name?"

"What is yours?"

"Tamara Petrovna Rogozina."

"Mine is Nick Carter."

The reaction was immediate. The fact that Carter fully intended to kill her had meant nothing. His real identity did. The eyes went dead and a white line appeared along her fine jaw.

"You know me?" he said, sipping his champagne and studying her over the rim of the glass.

"I have seen your file . . . in Moscow. We have code-named you 'Killmaster'."

Carter shrugged. "Then you know that if you are the genuine article, I can handle the problem and get you out."

"Yes, I do."

She gulped the rest of the glass. Carter poured two more, and she started to speak, all business now.

Her contact in Mannheim, West Germany, had given her all the details except her operations point in Paris.

Madonna had secured all the NATO information. Tamara had not been told all the exacts, but she was fairly sure that the information was somehow secreted inside, or on, the icon she was to help clear through customs.

"When is Madonna to arrive in Paris?"

"On the evening of the twenty-fifth. Another agent in Paris has already made reservations for him at the Ritz."

"The Ritz?"

"Yes. It seems he wants a last bourgeois fling in the West. My superiors are only too happy to give it to him, in light of the information he is bringing out. He is to contact me upon his arrival, and I am to inform him of my location. The morning of the twenty-sixth, he will check out of the Ritz and come to me in the flat."

"An apartment? . . . Not a hotel?"

"Yes."

"That could pose problems staying close to you."

"I know," she admitted, "but that is their way. I won't know the location of the place until I reach Paris. No one contact knows about another. Once Madonna is handed over to me, I take it from there, making sure he gets on the Aeroflot flight with the statue, or whatever it is.''

Carter was silent for several moments, smoking, letting his brain go its own way in putting the pieces together.

''You still have the Paris number?''

''Yes.''

''Use it as soon as you can after you reach the apartment. We have ways, no matter where it is, to offer your neighbors vacations they can't refuse. Do you think they will be watching you?''

''No, at least not until the contact with Madonna has been made. Then I am sure there will be some . . . what you call, backup . . . to make sure we get on the flight.''

Here she paused, her fingers suddenly rubbing nervously across the surface of the glass.

''There's something else?'' Carter murmured.

''Yes,'' she replied, the first note of insecurity creeping into her voice. ''There is a contingency, the real reason I was chosen.''

She paused, her features growing taut over the already prominent bones of her face. Whatever the contingency was, Carter thought, it must be very distasteful.

He didn't urge her to speak, preferring to let her take her own time. When she did continue, there was a stony hardness to her voice that didn't agree with the painful vulnerability that had crept into her eyes.

''In the Soviet Union, there is no good or evil. There is only the State. We are but servants of the State, our lives meant to be lived only for its propagation.''

''That pretty well sums up the Leninist philosophy,'' Carter intoned, and then made a guess. ''They want you to kill him.''

She nodded. ''If there is time between the hour of his arrival at the flat and departure for the flight to learn the secret of the Madonna, I am to seduce and kill him.''

''How?''

"I am trained with the needle stiletto, much like the one you had in your right hand when I entered the room."

Carter remembered the double agent Ahrens had mentioned in Berlin, and nodded. He stood and, grasping her hand, tugged her to her feet.

"If all goes well, Tamara Rogozina, there won't be any need for you to do any more killing."

The following afternoon, her call came into the Paris AXE hot line. The apartment was on rue Lepic, near the Place du Tertre and Sacré-Coeur in Montmartre.

Within six hours, a young widow and her two small daughters were enjoying the charms of a four-star hotel and the sun on the Riviera. Within twenty-four hours, carpenters had constructed an undetectable panel between the two apartments in the rear of the adjoining closets.

Tamara's apartment was watched constantly, and daily swept for bugs. Each evening, Carter or Norman Ahrens—who had been brought in from Berlin—would slip through the panel into the woman's apartment.

Ahrens's job was to brief her on the new identity and life the United States government was providing.

Carter's job was to debrief her concerning her own life, and go over, detail by detail, the capture and kidnap of Madonna when he arrived.

All had gone well until the previous afternoon, the twenty-fourth, the day before Madonna's arrival.

Carter had slipped through the panel as usual. He moved through the dark bedroom and on into the living room. It, too, was dark, the only illumination coming from the sodium streetlight outside.

Tamara stood at the window in a pale blue peignoir, her shoulders slumped. The gown was expensive, purchased by Ahrens from a Paris shop and given to her as a gift.

Now, with her arms hugging her body tightly beneath her small breasts and her head lowered in thought, Carter thought she looked like the original little-girl-lost.

"I made my last contact," she said without turning, "about two hours ago at the newsstand."

"And?"

"They are bringing in a backup . . . two, as a matter of fact. I was told it was only a cautionary procedure, in case I was not able to handle Madonna myself."

Then she did turn, and even in the dim light Carter could read the strain on her face and the harsh glare of hate in her eyes.

"But you don't believe them."

"No, I know them too well. They are taking every precaution. As soon as I have the information, I am to place a call. I would imagine the number they gave me rings a pay phone somewhere nearby, down there in Montmartre. They will come up here and handle the rest of it."

"Eliminate Madonna."

"Yes."

Suddenly she moved in close to Carter, her slender hands gripping the lapels of his jacket, her dark head resting against his chest.

"That's obviously not all of it," Carter growled, barely able to resist slipping his arms around her slender body.

"No. I think they mean to terminate me as well."

"Are you sure?"

"No."

"I don't believe in woman's intuition," Carter said, grasping her by the shoulders and holding her at arm's length.

"Neither do I," Tamara replied, now revealing the real depths of her fear by allowing her native accent to mar her usually near perfect English.

That alone told Carter that she meant what she said and had her own good reasons to believe it. She was good and she was well trained. And in the time they had spent together, Carter had learned that she didn't rattle easily.

But still he pushed. "How do you know?"

"I don't. It's just too big a change in plans at such a late date. I've gone over the last six months, hour by hour, in my mind, trying to remember if I have made any mistakes, given them a clue that I might be a traitor.''

"Defector," Carter said. "In this day and age, there's a difference. Did you remember anything?"

"Yes. Twice, I might have failed to cover myself completely while making contacts with your people. I thought I did, but I can't be sure."

"All right, I believe you. How much did they tell you about the two coming in?"

"They are Bulgarians. As you know, they are often used for this kind of work. They have already left Sofia for Athens; that much I was able to learn."

Carter's mind worked fast. The routes for Bulgarian assassins were known by AXE: straight down to Greece or across Yugoslavia, Albania, and the Adriatic Sea to Italy and Rome were the most common.

"I'll be back soon," he said.

Carter headed for the bedroom, and she followed, grasping him by the sleeve at the closet door.

"What are you going to do?"

"If we can spot them coming in, take them out before they can get to you . . . or to Madonna."

Agents and subagents in Athens, London, and Rome were alerted. The time factor ruled out auto or boat travel, so every airfield was covered.

No luck in Athens, but they were picked up in Rome. Charlie Weatherby, Carter's AXE contact in Paris, had roused Carter in the apartment an hour and a half earlier.

"Rome thinks they've got them, boarding an Air France flight to Paris due into Orly at five-fifty."

Carter checked his watch as he raised the glass of milky yellow liquid to his lips.

It was now 6:05.

Outside, it was raining heavily. Carter's eyes shifted to the rain-soaked windows. He watched planes line up for takeoff on one runway. Everything was late, departures and arrivals. The stack for departures was fourteen planes deep.

Carter felt a tightening in his gut. If the Air France flight from Rome was diverted to Switzerland or Brussels because of the weather, Carter and Company were in trouble. They wouldn't have enough time to shift the teams they had gathered for intercept to the frontiers.

He shifted his eyes to the two arrival runways. Planes were still landing in the billowing mist, their wheels creating a wide swath of water as they touched down.

Again Carter flipped his wrist upward. It was 6:42.

He was about to head toward the arrival area and do some checking on his own, when Charlie Weatherby's sallow face appeared above the stairs. Beneath the damply matted hair covering his narrow forehead, his eyes gleamed and his usually sullen lips were stretched in a smile.

Without a pause, he slid into a chair opposite Carter and pulled two Polaroid snaps from his pocket.

"I think we've got 'em. Took these at the baggage carousel."

Carter took the photos and leaned intently over them.

The first photo was of two men, both standing near the revolving carousel. One man had his back turned, the other was facing almost full into the camera.

He was a small man with black hair and a dark complexion. There was a sharp, ferretlike appearance to his face, and a hungry look in the dark eyes and thin, cruel lips. There was a tenseness in his body, as if he were waiting for something to happen.

Carter searched his memory, came up blank, and said so.

"Check the other pic," Weatherby said. "The second dude is turned around."

Carter did, and smiled.

The man was well over six feet, with wide, powerful shoulders that made him look even larger. He had a nice, boyishly friendly face and thick, curly hair that was probably dirty blond in the winter. Now it was so sun-bleached that it looked like it had come out of a bottle.

Carter's knuckles went white where he gripped the picture, but a wide grin creased his broad face.

"Androssov," he whispered.

"That's right, Yuri Androssov, in the flesh. One of their best, if not *the* best."

"It's a good thing I wasn't hanging around the gate. He would have spotted me in a minute."

Carter had come up against Androssov, the boyish-looking Bulgarian killer, twice in the past . . . in London and Geneva.

Both times it had been a draw.

This time it would be different. It had to be.

"Not much doubt about what they're here for," Weatherby said, a little cackle in his otherwise bland voice.

"None." Carter nodded. "Where are they now?"

"Getting through customs. I've managed to hold them up for a little bit. They're both traveling under Italian passports, obviously phony. The short, scared one is Leonetti on his passport. Androssov is Pietro della Scala."

Carter chuckled. "That fits his flair. Are the teams ready?"

"All set," Weatherby replied. "We've got two spotters on the walk, and three cabs ready to move in line when our boys' turn comes up. We should have a ninety-nine-percent chance of steering them into at least one of them. If they have a car waiting, we've got three unmarked civilians—a Citroën, and two brands of Renault—to pick up the tail."

"Then let's go!" Carter said, rising.

FIVE

Weatherby drove the big Citroën like a man possessed. He knew every boulevard, back street, and alley in Paris, and he moved through them like the coachman of Louis XVI: *Get the hell out of my way, Royalty coming through!*

"Check four-twenty-one again!"

Carter grabbed the hand mike and barked a location request to car 421.

"I unloaded them near the Porte d'Orléans, on the Boulevard Romain-Rolland."

"Were you able to plant the beeper?"

"*Non.* Sorry, they grabbed their own bags before I could get my hands on them."

"Were four-twenty or four-twenty-two on the scene?"

"Yes, I'm sure one of them cruised the subjects, but who got them, I don't know."

"Check. Out," Carter said, and turned to Weatherby.

"Check the other two channels."

"Dammit," Carter muttered, and he began dialing.

Everything had gone well at the airport. Yuri Androssov had been steered into the second of the three cabs, 421. Cab 420 had faked engine trouble and dumped his fare within a mile of Orly; 422 had pulled out of line and stayed with 421.

The plan was for the two cabs to shadow the target cab and be available if the targets did a switch. It had worked,

39

obviously, but which of the two cabs had the passengers, and in what direction were they heading?

Both of the other channels were quiet.

"Play dispatcher and call them up for a destination and an ETA," Weatherby said, cruising the perimeter of the Montrouge Cemetery for the third time.

Carter chose 420, and the driver replied instantly.

"Four-twenty-two has them. They headed back toward the Seine. I lost them on Avenue du Général-Leclerc, at the Fontaine Observatory."

Weatherby hung a hard left and jerked Carter's neck against the headrest as the Citroën hurtled back toward the center of Paris.

"They're playing games," he hissed, weaving through traffic like a madman.

"Obviously," the Killmaster replied and punched the button on the hand mike. "Four-twenty?"

"Oui, monsieur" came the calm reply.

"Move your ass to St.-Michel and St.-Germain. You might pick them up if we miss them."

"Oui, monsieur."

Carter turned back to Weatherby. "What do you think?"

"I don't think they're heading for a hotel."

"Obviously. If they switch cabs again, we're in trouble."

"You might say that. Check these cab numbers as I pass them. And shield your face."

They were at the traffic circle in front of the Fontaine Observatory. Carter checked each number as Weatherby bulled his way past a long line of cabs.

"Nothing," Carter said, flipping the channel receiver to the one allotted to 422.

They were at the Place St.-Michel, double-parked on the Seine side, when the radio crackled and a voice finally found its way through the static.

"Four-twenty-two to base . . . four-twenty-two to base . . ."

"Base here, four-twenty-two. Are you engaged?"

"No. I dropped them at rue de Chanaleilles, between Barbet-de-Jouy and rue Vaneau."

"And . . . ?"

"It's an alley of bistros and shops. I made a clear loop and watched them come out on the Vaneau side. They got in a blue Renault Five four-door, license number 500X5-864B, and headed toward the Right Bank over the Pont de la Concorde. I couldn't chance following them farther than that."

Weatherby had already made a U-turn and crossed the Seine before 422 had finished his spiel. He caught Carter's glance and shrugged. "Ask him."

"Four-twenty-two?"

"Still here."

"Were you able to plant a beeper?"

"Yes, sir" came the reply, bringing a sigh of relief to both men in the speeding Citroën. "It's stuck under the pocket flap of the short one's jacket."

"Lovely job, four-twenty-two. Go home," Carter cried and killed the two-way.

In the same motion, he flipped on the HF-DF receiver. A green map of Paris floated onto the dash screen, crisscrossed by yellow, blue, and pink lines.

Within seconds a white blip appeared, bobbing in a straight direction.

"They just turned north off the Champs-Élysées."

"Rue de Berri. Got it. Hang on!"

The Citroën again gained wings, and seat belt or no, Carter found himself being alternately thrown against the door and hanging on for dear life to keep from colliding against Weatherby on left-hand turns.

"You're closing fast," Carter said.

"Don't I know it. Don't worry, chum, I've got one eye on the screen and one on the road."

Carter hung on and chuckled. Weatherby was a good man. He most probably knew Paris better than the vast majority of its inhabitants and was a master of slang in four languages.

He didn't have "N" status with AXE—a license to kill—but Carter was as at ease with him as he had ever been with any other agent he respected.

Another five minutes and several more hair-raising turns brought them onto the rue des Dames.

"They're heading for the Montmartre Cemetery!"

Weatherby nodded, his face set in rigid lines. "I doubt if they have a nest on top of our lady pigeon, though. Close, maybe, but not in the same building."

"There they are!" Carter yelled, his eyes registering the license number as well as the make and model of the car.

"Drop! I'm going on around them."

Just as Carter unhooked his seat belt and slid to the floor, the little Renault crawled into a parking space. Seconds later, Weatherby two-wheeled the Citroën into an alley and jumped out.

"Stay out of sight!"

Carter also exited the car but remained in the cover of the alley. He lit a cigarette and watched Weatherby's progress.

The agent darted into a flower shop and emerged in seconds with an armful of roses. Passing a newsstand, he lifted a paper, dropping coins in payment without pausing, and was soon halfway down the block directly opposite the Renault.

Androssov and his little friend were just entering a building two numbers back from the car.

Weatherby passed the house, doubled back to recheck the number, and rejoined Carter.

"It's rue Louie Pais, number one-sixty-eight."

"What do you think? . . . safe house?"

Weatherby nodded. "The stairs are directly in front. I watched them go to the top . . . that would be the sixth floor."

"Get on the horn," Carter said. "Have the whole block covered, but use men who know how to be invisible."

"I have no other kind," Weatherby chuckled.

"And get me a floor plan of the house, all the way back to Napoleon, if possible."

"Do we take them?"

"As soon as it's dark," Carter replied, already moving toward a phone booth he had spotted at the other end of the alley.

Tamara answered on the first ring.

"Madame Dumain?"

"I'm afraid you have the wrong number."

"*Pardon, madame, pardon.*"

Carter hung up the phone and lit a cigarette. When he was sure she had had enough time to slip through the closet into the other apartment, he dialed that number.

The rooms and the phone in her apartment were swept daily for bugs, but too much was at stake to take even the smallest chance.

"Nick?" Her voice was tense but controlled.

"Yeah. We picked them up at Orly. They came to roost in a safe house. Don't worry—by midnight they'll be out of it. Any word yet?"

"He's in, under his own name at the Ritz. I called back to check after he made contact."

"Anything to add?"

"Nothing. I gave him this address, he thanked me and said that I could expect him at ten o'clock in the morning."

"Good enough. We'll let him have his night on the town and hit him the second you get him inside the apartment in the morning. You calm?"

"Yes, now that it is almost over."

"Have a meal sent up. I'll drop in and kiss you good night when I'm finished here."

"I'd like that."

Carter hung up and headed back down the alley.

The way she had said "I'd like that" was echoing in the back of his head.

She had said a lot with just three words, and he suddenly realized how fond of her he had become.

Julian Carmont emerged from the elaborately tiled Ritz

bathroom, patting after shave lotion on his face. He winced slightly as the astringent bit into his cheeks, and slid his arms into a summer-weight gray cashmere jacket. Like the jacket, the off-white silk shirt and the dark blue trousers had been tailored to his precise specifications in London.

Carmont never bought clothes off the rack. Tailored clothes and Italian-made shoes were part of his carefully cultivated image.

Julian Carmont lived well, and after the coming night's work, he expected to live even better.

He moved to a wall mirror and carefully brushed his hair with two silver-backed brushes.

Unabashedly, he admired the tanned skin and clean, aristocratic lines of his face. Beneath the jacket, he could feel the supple roll of his shoulder, back, and arm muscles.

Carmont was forty-five, but he had kept his body as trim as a man half that age.

His face and his body were half his fortune. His brains were the other half. And tonight they would all work together to give him financial security for the rest of his life.

He set the brushes down and moved from the mirror to the bed. Carefully, he checked and then rechecked the contents of the briefcase, then snapped it shut.

As he passed his bag on the way to the door, he checked its locks. It wouldn't do for an inquisitive maid to idly peruse the bag's belongings. Not that any chambermaid at the Ritz would even think of doing such a thing, but Julian Carmont took no chances.

He shunned the elevator and walked four floors down to the lobby. At the first floor he paused, lighting a cigarette.

At his left was the main entrance to the hotel from the Place Vendôme. Directly across was the upper lounge. It was a piano bar, tastefully done in soft leather, old wood, and spongy carpets.

It closed at 2 A.M.

Around the corner to his far left was the small, main reception area. After midnight it was manned by the night concierge, a computer-trained auditor, and a switchboard operator.

Just to the rear of the desk, behind the key and mail slots, was the auditor and switchboard operator's work area, as well as the two hotel safes. At the far end of the desk was an ordinary wooden door leading to a narrow room containing the hotel's safe-deposit boxes.

At midnight, that door was closed and locked, and the keys were placed in the larger of the hotel safes.

Carmont chuckled to himself as he turned right and strolled down the long arcade lined with exquisite display cases representing over a hundred of the leading boutiques and jewelers of Paris.

The cases, like the door to the safe-deposit-box room and the safes, would be child's play for Pierre Donet.

Idly, Carmont's eyes drifted to the sparkling gems in cases emblazoned with names like Cartier, Baccarat, Fred, and Van Cleef & Arpels.

All the gems on display were real, of course.

After all, this was the Ritz.

Between the banks of cases on his right were salons and private rooms for conferences, private party areas for drinks, and even more private rooms for the very rich to dine with the very rich away from the prying eyes of those who were only moderately rich.

To his left were more doors leading into a courtyard and twin, immaculately maintained inner gardens. Those doors would be closed and locked between midnight and one o'clock.

At the end of the hall, he turned right and then left to pass by the elegant Espadon Grill. Adjacent to the dining room was the intimate Hemingway Bar, and across from it, to Carmont's left, a lounge/sitting room of antique sofas and chairs, some of them dating from the reign of one or the other Louis.

At midnight the dining rooms closed, and one hour later the bar followed suit. By two o'clock, receipts from the bars and dining rooms were gathered and placed in the larger hotel safe.

The rear of the hotel led out to the very narrow rue Cambon. It was locked at two o'clock, forcing any late revelers to enter through the main, Place Vendôme entrance.

Carmont was whistling lightly as he stepped onto the rue Cambon and turned left. His stride was long and sure but unhurried as he turned right onto rue St.-Honoré, and then left onto rue Royale and the Place de la Concorde.

As he walked through the entrance to the Crillon Hotel, he checked his watch. It was eight o'clock.

Seven and a half hours until go.

Marta Penn stared out from the Crillon suite's window. Barely six blocks away, she could see the curved buildings of the Place Vendôme and the rear of the Ritz.

It had been seven hours since her arrival in Paris with the drunk and the whore. Since then, she had adhered to Carmont's plan to the letter. She had not left the suite, nor had she failed to check on the other two in the suite next door every fifteen minutes.

She was about to freshen her drink, when a light, irregular tap came from the hall door. The manner told her who it was, but she left the chain on anyway.

"Cautious, my dear?" Carmont whispered through the crack. "That's very good."

He glided past her down the three steps into the suite, dropping his briefcase on a coffee table and lowering his body to the thickly cushioned sofa.

"I hope that's only wine," he commented, inclining his head toward the glass in her hand.

"It is," Marta replied curtly. "I am not a female Dino Foche. Would you like a glass?"

"Please." He nodded, leaning forward and unlocking the briefcase. "Where are they, by the way?"

"In the next suite. He's sleeping. I think Claudia is taking a bath."

"How are her nerves?"

"No better, no worse, but she'll make it."

"How can you be so sure?" Carmont asked, removing articles from the briefcase.

"Because if she doesn't, I told her I would kill her. Here."

"Then I'm sure she will do quite well," Carmont said, accepting the glass and patting the sofa beside him. "Let's go over everything one more time."

Marta sat, her eyes scanning the items on the coffee table. There were three microminiaturized walkie-talkies, with Velcro backs. Marta knew there would be matching pieces of Velcro on the front of the three jump suits also on the table. Also attached to the collar of the jump suits were white, elasticized hoods with eye and nose holes cut into the faces.

Her eyes moved to a can of chloroform, a tear gas gun, three pairs of infrared night glasses that appeared to be no more than stylish sunglasses, and a broken-down 9mm Beretta with a three-inch silencer.

"Do you think that will be necessary?" she murmured, motioning to the Beretta.

Carmont shrugged. "We take no chances. Needless to say, these items—the Beretta, the tear gas gun, and this—are strictly for your use."

Into Marta's hand he dropped a piece of flat, spring steel about six inches long and a half inch wide. Three inches of one side had been sharpened to a razor's edge. The other three inches were wrapped with a thin but very strong nylon thread to serve as a handle. It made the whole a flat but very effective knife: quick, silent, and extremely deadly.

Besides its effectiveness, both the sharp tip and blunt edge could be used as lever and pick for window and door locks.

It was designed to be carried between the layers of a belt or in a boot or shoe. The flexibility of the steel allowed it to bend around the waist or adhere to the movements of a foot or leg.

"Bring back memories?"

Marta nodded and let a humorless smile crease her lips. A little more than a year earlier, on Malta, she had used just such a weapon to enter a hotel room and slit a sleeping man's throat.

"Let's hope you won't need it," Carmont said.

"Of course. Let's get on with it."

He spread two maps on the table—one of Paris and one of the Ritz's interior—and, for the fiftieth time, went over the details of the robbery.

At one-thirty, Marta, Claudia, and Dino—all dressed in evening clothes—were to enter the lower lounge of the Ritz on the rue Cambon side and order drinks, Perrier for Dino. The women were not to remove their gloves, and Marta must remember to wipe Dino's glass before they left.

At the main bank of elevators, they would kiss each other and loudly say their good nights. Marta and Claudia would get off at the mezzanine and enter the women's powder room, where they would change and remain until 3:28.

Dino would remain in the elevator to the VIP floor. At 1:45, Carmont would have summoned the night porter to his suite and sent him down for sandwiches. The porter's room beside the maid's room would be empty. Dino was to hide in there until 3:20, when he would use the chloroform on the porter and then join Carmont.

"Do you have it all?"

"I had it two months ago," Marta replied.

"How about execution and getaway?"

"The same."

Carmont shrugged. "Good enough. Pierre is briefing the others on the barge. I should be getting back."

Marta followed him to the door. "How much do you think we'll clean?"

"About a quarter of a million in cash right away for you, Pierre, and myself. When the heat cools off and the rest is fenced . . . who knows? I would guess another million and a half apiece."

"Dollars or francs?"

"Dollars, my darling. With the exchange rate the way it is, I deal only in dollars, you know that."

Marta was smiling as she closed the door behind him. Suddenly it didn't really matter that her long affair with Julian Carmont was almost over.

She had already picked out her retirement spot, and once there, she knew she would meet another Julian Carmont.

SIX

Carter checked his face in the mirror, and then the back of his hands. The lampblack did a good job. If there was a glare of light, no skin would show.

He had traded his jacket and shirt for a black turtleneck, and pulled a black knit seaman's cap down over his head past his ears.

"You sure you want to solo this?" Weatherby asked from the driver's seat beside him.

"You got a better idea?" Carter replied. "Like you joining me, for instance?"

The other man looked down at the paunch of his belly where it nestled the steering wheel, and chuckled. "I guess you're right."

"Everything covered?"

Weatherby nodded. "Six men on the exits and two more on the roof. They've got lines to haul you up."

"Good enough," Carter said and checked his hardware.

Hugo was in his chamois sheath beneath the sleeve of the sweater. Wilhelmina, his 9mm Luger complete with silencer, was nestled against his spine under his belt.

Hopefully, the Luger wouldn't be needed.

He also had a long-barreled .22 specially rigged to fire rubber bullets tipped with plastic caps. On impact, the plastic cap would disintegrate and the substance inside the bullet would spread through the blood in seconds, knocking out its receiver.

"How about the phony ambulance?"

"Ready to roll, complete with two little men in white coats. We've got our own safe house, about twelve miles south on the highway to Orléans. We can keep them there for the duration."

Carter nodded and slipped from the car. On sneakered feet he moved into an alley and jogged to the first corner. There he turned right and counted off the dark backs of the buildings until he found number 168.

The rain had let up to a drizzle, but, thankfully, ugly black and gray clouds still covered the Paris sky, blotting out whatever moonlight might be trying to get through.

By finger feel, he worked his way along a high board fence until he found both the gate and its latch. Before lifting it, he squinted his eyes to see through a crack in the boards.

The entire house had been remodeled less than three years before by an architect/contractor named Lodolphin. It was six stories high, and each of the three apartments contained two floors, front to back.

The architect had retained the first duplex apartment for himself. The second was occupied by an attorney, his wife and two children. The third had been purchased by a Hungarian petrochemical company as a Paris placc for visiting party executives and customers.

The middle two floors were dark. The other four blazed with light, even though it was past midnight.

Carter gently lifted the latch, slipped through the gate, and quietly closed it behind him. He trotted past a small shed, probably used to store gardening tools, and then slowed to a crawl when the sandy path beneath his shoes turned to gravel.

A scurrying sound to his right near the corner of the house brought him up short. He dropped to one knee and lifted the dart pistol, moving its muzzle back and forth across the shadows of thick bushes and low-cut trees.

The sound came again, and then a gold and white tabby

came sauntering out from under one of the bushes. He came right up to Carter and purred as loudly as a diesel engine as he ran the length of his furry body along the Killmaster's leg.

"Nice pussy, go home . . . wherever it is."

As if in answer, the rear terrace door of the lower apartment opened, bathing the garden just in front of Carter in light.

The Killmaster was about to slip farther back into the darkness, when a tall, graying man in a robe and slippers stepped from the door.

"Minou! *Le diner est servi!*"

Carter pushed the big tabby up the path, and when Minou refused to go farther, he tapped him on the rump with the palm of his hand.

It was useless. The cat only skittered around his hands, back to Carter's leg, and purred even louder.

"Minou!" the man called again and came down the two remaining steps to the garden.

Carter froze, but before he could take any action, the man changed his mind. He retraced his steps into the house, and seconds later the sound of an electric can opener reached the lurking Killmaster's ears.

It also reached the cat. With a low growling purr, he took off across the garden, up the steps, and bounded into the house.

Carter waited a few more moments, during which the rear door was closed and the rear lights in the lower apartment were extinguished.

With a sigh of relief he moved forward, tugging a tiny penlight from his pocket. Still several feet from the house, he pointed the light upward and flashed it twice.

Two flashes, far to his left, came back instantly. He cut that way and almost collided with a one-inch line spiraling down from the roof.

The two men on the roof had chosen the spot well. Carter, in the darkness, hadn't spotted a slight indentation in the brick. It was probably made by adjoining fireplaces in back-to-back rooms all the way up through the three apartments. From between them, it was almost impossible to see Carter going up, hand over hand, and there were no windows of any kind in the indentation itself.

Past the second floor, he slowed, and then barely crawled as he came up over the ledge of the fifth floor. Once he had gained a foothold, he stopped and listened.

There were lights in the rooms to his right and left. But to the right he could hear voices, female voices.

Releasing the rope and digging his fingers into the crevices between the bricks, he moved. Inches short of the open window, he stopped, crouched, and carefully edged an eye around the sill.

The room was French modern and done in tastefully muted colors.

The two women occupying it were anything but muted.

One was in red spike heels and red stockings, complete with matching merry widow. The tightly cinched corset had made an hourglass out of her righly endowed figure and forced the biggest portion of the sand out over the top.

The other was just pulling a black, skintight leather dress over a similar rig. While not as endowed as her sister, this one had more in the body department than most women would ever hope to acquire.

But while the bodies were more than interesting, it was the hair and faces that drew Carter's attention to the point of fascination.

The one in leather had spiky purple hair standing at least a foot above her head. The other had the same ''do,'' only in a garish emerald green and utilizing about twice as many spikes.

The faces looked like demonstrations for new makeup, all colors from blue to purple to green to garish red, with a chalky white base.

They were speaking in Russian with some Georgian dialect, which Carter could understand.

''Are you nearly ready?''

"Almost," Green Hair replied, "if I can just get all of me into this."

It was satiny, short, and a green that almost matched her hair. She did manage to get all of her into it, but just barely.

"Shall I put the kit in my purse or yours?"

"Yours. I have the gun in mine."

"Was that the phone?"

"Yes, one of them will get it."

Carter listened to their chatter for another thirty seconds and started to edge his way back to the line, when Androssov himself suddenly walked into the room.

"Good God, both of you look like Pigalle whores!"

"Not whores, Yuri," Purple Hair replied, "punk. It's the youth look, and according to Control, he leans toward youth. Who was on the phone?"

"Maurice. Our man picked up the Lido reservation. You have the table right next to his. You'd better hurry, it's the one o'clock show."

"We're ready."

"Phone me from the hotel the minute you have it. We can move yet tonight if everything goes well."

"And if we don't get it?"

Androssov shrugged. "That's why we have a backup."

Little bells went off in the back of Carter's mind. Were they going after Almar Koenigburger tonight? It would fit . . . a *double* double cross.

But first things first.

As soon as Androssov and the two women left the room, Carter slipped through the window. Quickly, he moved to the door and cracked it.

He could hear their voices from somewhere far to his left, and then a door slamming. He guessed that the footsteps returning were the Bulgarian's and closed the door to the barest crack.

When the light was blocked out by the Bulgarian's passing body, Carter counted a short two, swung the door wide, and brought the altered .22 up in both hands.

The man's instincts and speed were remarkable. He rolled to the side, toward the wall, just as Carter fired. The rubber pellet whined uselessly along the ceiling and thudded into a door at the end of the hall.

Androssov used his shoulder against the wall as a fulcrum and threw himself into the Killmaster's legs. The jolt was solid, enough to trip him but not enough to dislodge the gun. Carter brought it back into play just as the other man rolled to one knee, bringing up a silenced Walther from the small of his back.

Both men fired at the same time.

Carter felt a tug at his left side and, almost instantly, the burning sensation he knew was the aftermath of the passing slug. He knew that the Walther slug had either passed clean through him, or, hopefully, had just taken a little skin. He heard the lead thud into the wall to his left.

Androssov caught it all, plastic tip and rubber bullet, dead in the center of his chest.

His eyes went wide and he staggered back.

"Leonid . . . Nadia!" he gasped, his full lips popping open and closing like a dying fish as he grasped the Walther with both hands, trying to lift it for a second shot.

The chemical substance was working, but just in case, Carter slipped sideways before moving forward. When he was beside the other man, he chopped down with the .22 across Androssov's wrist.

There were two loud thuds: first, the Walther hitting the floor, and second, Androssov's body.

But there were other noises, lots of them, and all at once: doors opening and footsteps pounding down from the top floor of the duplex.

"Yuri . . ."

The smaller Bulgarian swung around the corner and came to an abrupt halt in the hallway. He took everything in with one glance and came up with a Walther of his own.

It was a long hall, at least twenty-five yards.

Carter knew the little .22 was not worth a damn beyond ten

feet for accuracy. And at twenty-five yards, the velocity
might not even be enough for penetration.

There was only time for a split-second decision, and he
made it in less time than that.

Dropping the .22, he raced full steam forward toward the
smaller man and clawed Wilhelmina from the small of his
back at the same time.

He hit the floor as the man fired. The first slug went
harmlessly over his head. A second one tore into the
hardwood by his shoulder, and Carter fired twice himself,
point-blank.

Wilhelmina's first slug spun the Bulgarian back against the
wall. The second took him in the side, at an upward angle,
and killed.

Carter heard the scrape of a boot behind him and remembered the other sound he had heard when Androssov's
drugged body hit the floor: a door opening.

He heard the first spitting sound of the .22 as he rolled to
his back and raked the hall behind him with his eyes.

She was a crone, with wild, graying hair, a pinched, aged,
wrinkled face, a gaudily flowered housecoat flapping at her
spindly legs, and murder in her eye.

Goddammit, Carter thought. First there were two, then
there were four, and now five.

The crone, evidently weaponless herself when she had
stepped through the door at the opposite end of the hall from
the current carnage, had picked up the .22 pellet pistol. It
held six sleepy-time pellets. Carter had fired two. Now, with
the tiny gun held like a lance in both hands before her
contorted face, she was wildly firing the other four at Carter.

He raised Wilhelmina, paused a millisecond too long as he
took in her wrinkled face and aging body, and then felt a
jarring pain in the same side where he had been wounded
already by Androssov.

She was directly above him now, the cylinder of the .22
whirling, the hammer falling on empty chambers. He saw the
frustration in her face, and then he saw her flip the gun in her

hands. As small as the .22 was, it still looked like the most
deadly piece of steel Carter had ever seen as, with a ven-
geance, she raised it above her head and started to bring it
down with all the force in her frail arms directly at his head.

He had no choice.

He could feel the chemical substance from her one sure
shot spreading throughout his body.

With a groan, he brought the silenced muzzle of the Luger
upward and began firing.

Almar Koenigburger's eyes gleamed and the old familiar
tingling sensation was already surging through his crotch.

What luck, what incomparable luck. He silently thanked
whomever his contact control had been for dropping the Lido
ticket off for him at the Ritz desk. He could only thank
Providence for the coincidence of the two girls at the adjoining table.

They were young and garish and their dress was almost
lewd.

Koenigburger had initiated the conversation just before the
show had started. Both women had responded, particularly
the voluptuous one with the green hair.

Even with all the seminudity on the stage, the old man's
eyes kept moving toward the straining front of that green
dress. He could vividly imagine what lay beneath, and what it
would be like to run his hands and lips over that warm,
yielding flesh.

They thanked him with their eyes for the drinks he sent
over during the show and eagerly accepted an offer to join
him for another when it was over.

Their names were Nanette and Babette. They were stu-
dents, and, yes, it was very expensive to get an education
these days.

Their eyes lit up with anticipation when Koenigburger
mentioned that he was staying at the Ritz, in a suite.

His eyes lit up when he felt the green-haired girl's—

Babette—gentle hand on his leg under the table.

"Would *monsieur* like some company in his suite this evening?"

"Indeed I would," he replied, his eyes darting questioningly at the other girl.

With a smile, Nanette leaned forward and answered the question in his eyes herself. "Surely, if *monsieur* has a suite at the Ritz he can afford to help *two* struggling girls further their education?"

Koenigburger was shaking like a teen-ager about to indulge in his first sexual experience.

"I cannot see where that would be a problem at all."

He paid the bill for both tables, and arm in arm, the three of them left the Lido.

Koenigburger glanced at his watch. It was just two-thirty.

He was to meet his contact at her apartment at ten in the morning.

He would use every minute. Who needed sleep? He could sleep on the flight to Moscow.

Julian Carmont fastened the tool belt around his middle and screwed a silencer onto the muzzle of a Beretta. He slid the pistol into a makeshift holster on the belt, then pulled a hood up to cover his head and face.

He placed the steel kit containing the laser drill near the door, and then returned to the bed and picked up the two-way walkie-talkie. The antenna slid out easily, and there was barely any static as he checked both "send" and "receive."

When he was satisfied, he adjusted the frequency and depressed the "send" button.

"Ladies?"

"We're here" came Marta's voice, loud and clear.

"Any problems?"

"None. Dino should be in place by now."

Carmont depressed the "warn" button on the set, and a red light glowed near the speaker. Hopefully, somewhere near the end of the hall in the storage room beside the night porter's cubicle, a matching red light would also be glowing on Dino's set.

And if it did . . . .

It did. Two seconds later, Dino had pushed his own "warn" button and a green light blinked on beside the red on Julian's set.

"He's in and ready," Julian growled. "Pierre?"

"Here. Carmine and I are parked in the limousine on Capucines, just outside the Place Vendôme entrance."

"Excellent. Alain?"

"Here. We are under the loading dock just outside the service entrance door."

"The security guard will unlock the door for the night janitors to put out the garbage in ten minutes. Be ready!"

"No problem."

"And be sure," Carmont intoned, lowering his voice, "be very sure that *all* the garbage cans are out before you take them."

A low chuckle came from the set, and then Alain Mittain's gravelly voice came on. "Have I ever been less than perfect on a job, Julian?"

It was Carmont's turn to chuckle. "No, Alain, you haven't, and neither have the rest of us. That is why we have never seen the inside of a prison." Then the humor went out of his voice. "Let us not make an exception in this case. Everyone listen . . . we go in fifteen minutes."

Almar Koenigburger stood at the foot of the bed. He had kicked off his shoes and cast aside his shirt. Perspiration dripped from his half-naked body.

Somewhere behind him, in the bathroom, the one with the purple hair was doing something.

But the old man didn't care what that one was doing. He was mesmerized by the erotic sight of Babette shedding her green dress.

Her garishly painted mouth was in a pout, and Almar could swear that her heavily mascaraed eyes were flashing up at him with the same degree of lust he knew could be seen in his.

"Beautiful, my dear, my God, but you are a vision. Take the rest of it off as well."

She writhed her arms up toward the center of her breasts, and the old man gasped in anticipation as her fingers tugged at the laces of her merry widow.

"Yes . . . yes," he panted.

She came up toward him, smiling as her breasts spilled from the garment. Then her nipples touched him. He heard a sound behind him, but he paid no attention. His whole being was riveted on the sensations coursing through his body as her breasts pillowed across his chest.

Her arms encircled his neck, and suddenly he was being tugged down to the bed, over her body, between her long, powerful legs.

"My trousers . . . let me remove . . ."

"Soon, *monsieur*."

The grip on his neck increased and her legs scissored around him, holding his body tightly to hers.

"*Ach, was ist . . .*"

A biting pain struck his right shoulder, and a second later another needle was driven into his left shoulder.

Crying out, Almar Koenigburger began to kick and squirm. Desperately he tried to lift his hands up between their bodies and bring them to bear on her throat.

"Hold him."

"I am. Get his arms."

He felt his wrists being pulled back and twisted.

"How long does it take?"

"About a minute. Hang on, it won't be long now."

Another thirty seconds, and the green-haired girl relaxed her grip slightly as a test.

"I think he's out. Check the pulse. Well?"

"He's out. Roll him over."

Ten minutes later, through the fog that had clouded Almar Koenigburger's brain, he was describing, in detail, the secrets of the Madonna and its present location.

SEVEN

Charles Portain closed the door of the main safe and spun the dial several times.

To his left, he heard the new night switchboard operator slide into her chair.

Her name was Noelle Massmen, and since she had started on the job one week earlier, Portain had been trying to lure her upstairs to one of the vacant rooms during midshift.

He stood, adjusted his tie, and tidied a stray strand of his long black hair. Portain was a tall man of thirty-six, conventionally good-looking in an unspectacular way. He had a square-cut face and a body that he kept in good condition.

He had been night concierge at the Ritz for seven years out of choice. His wife was fat, over forty, and a shrew. By working nights, Charles could sleep days and rarely had to see or speak to his wife.

Out of the corner of his eye, he scrutinized the youthful Noelle Massmen. He couldn't exactly pinpoint what it was about the girl that made his blood flow faster. Her nose was longer than it should be, and her lips were thinner. Her chin was much too aggressive, and she was a little thinner than Portain preferred in the women he chose for extramarital affairs.

He decided that her breasts were shaped perfectly for a body like hers and that her melting brown eyes were the best feature in her face. Her hair was midnight black, and she seemed to have combed it straight back and done absolutely nothing else to it.

She was also totally in awe of any authority. Charles Portain was authority.

"Noelle . . ."

"*Oui, Monsieur Portain?*"

"*Charles, s'il vous plaît.*"

"*Oui,*" she said, smiling and leaning back in her chair to emphasize her small but perfect breasts.

Portain sat in the chair beside her and turned so that their knees touched.

"Do you remember my little suggestion last night?"

"I do, Charles."

"I think that tonight . . . or rather, this morning . . . would be good. We can take our break together at four."

The thin lips smiled, revealing crooked but very white teeth. "Will Madame Crossett mind watching the desk?"

Madame Crossett was the night auditor. She had known Charles Portain for five years and had always covered for him when he found an occasion to use one of the vacant rooms during their shift.

In return, Charles corrected her endless mistakes and never reported her gross incompetence.

"I don't think that will be a problem. Shall we say four . . . room four-ten?"

"Four in four-ten it is."

Charles reached forward with one hand to lightly caress her breast, when a sound in the outer reception area caught his attention.

"Till then, my dear."

He stood and moved around the partition, only to come up short behind the desk.

There were four of them. They all wore white jump suits, with white hoods over their heads and faces.

The tallest of the four held a pistol, its muzzle aimed directly at Charles Portain's face.

"It is loaded and very deadly, *monsieur*. But I assure you that if you and your fellow employees do exactly as I say, no one will be harmed."

It started far off, somewhere at the other end of another universe, wherever that might be. Resembling fragments of quivering crimson jelly, they rushed at him. Then they grew in size until they were huge, blood-red balloons.

Then they hit his brain, and the backs of his eyes burst into tiny pieces, each hammering every nerve ending in his body.

So this is it, thought Carter. *At last I've found out what it's like to be dead.*

A voice came out of the dark void that preceded the next set of red balloons: "He's awake. Or at least he's moving."

Carter wondered if it was Gabriel. *Don't blow your horn, Gabe, you'll split my skull in half.*

He felt himself swimming upward through the maze, but that didn't stop the balloons. It only made them worse.

He experimented by moving one finger, then two, and then his foot.

It worked. He actually experienced movement along with all the pain.

Hot damn, he thought, *I think I'm alive. By intense concentration I will now open my eyes and all the balloons will go away.*

The eyelids flickered and opened. Everything was hazy. Slowly, very slowly, objects began to focus. His eyes blinked the room into reality. It took on color and form, faces and bodies that whirled and grimaced and did headstands.

He snapped the protective eyelids shut again.

The balloons were better.

"Nick, Nick, are you awake? Can you hear me?"

You have a lovely, sweet voice, child. Please don't scream like that.

He was about to try again, when soft fingers, dipped in something cold and damp, greased his fevered brow.

Gently, child, gently. I'm dying.

His eyes opened again, only tiny slits. Her face was in two uneven parts, with one eye inches above the other, and she had four nostrils.

Slowly, with a lot of concentration and an equal degree of blinking, he brought the two halves together.

There was fear and concern in Tamara Petrovna's dark eyes. He also saw open vulnerability in the sweetly pleasant face.

That's nice, he thought, *a Russian agent who is also a killer has vulnerability. Anything is still possible in this world.*

And then he remembered she was on his side. Or supposed to be.

"Tamara . . ."

"Good, you recognize me."

Suddenly her face was gone. It was replaced with a broad, masculine one with a Gallic nose, watery eyes, and a mustache.

"Bring Tamara back. You look like somebody I should have shot ten years ago."

"I'm a doctor. How many fingers?"

"Where?"

"Open your eyes."

"Oh. Three . . . no, four."

"Good. Where are you?"

Carter flattened his palms and felt the soft smoothness of a sheet. "On a bed."

"No, I mean, what city?"

He had to think. And then he remembered. "Paris . . . Oh, Christ."

He tried to sit up, and the jelly balloons came back with his eyes open. Pain, hot and intense, spread from the vicinity of his left side and hit his brain like charging bolts of fire.

"Lie down."

He was shoved back, not too gently, and Tamara's face took the doctor's place. Her fingers went to work again, and Carter forced his mind and body to relax.

"The drug should wear off in another few minutes. He'll be groggy from the stimulants combating it, but he should be completely alert in a half hour or so."

"What about the wound?" The new voice was Weatherby's.

"From the scars on his body, somebody else has patched up a lot worse. This was just a scratch by comparison."

Carter heard a door close, and then Weatherby's face appeared alongside Tamara's above him.

"You're gonna live to get shot another day, old hoss."

"Thanks."

"Want to give me a rundown?"

Carter did, quickly, with as few words as possible. "The bitch of it was, there were five instead of two of them in there. What's the body count?"

"Two dead. Leonid Droposki, Pole works out of Bulgaria on special teams. The old lady was Nadia Podnerkov. You bagged a big one there. She was probably the control on the operation."

"And Androssov?"

"Still out. He's in the safe house south of Paris. We followed the two punk whores when they left. Nothing there. My men checked them into the Lido, and then came back. We figured they were prime-time diversion for Yuri and Leonid."

Punk whores.

The Lido.

Suddenly it all came back, including his mini-conclusions.

Again Carter started up, and this time he reached a sitting position without the top of his head coming off.

"They weren't whores. They were part of the team."

"What?"

"That's right. I overheard part of their conversation while they were dressing. They had somebody set up at the Lido. My guess is it was Koenigburger. I think they were going to try for the Madonna tonight, and use Tamara only for backup tomorrow if they missed."

Until then, Tamara had been silent. Now she spoke with a dry rasp in her voice. "I should have suspected. They planned to use me only in an emergency, or perhaps, if they guessed that I was coming over, not at all. I was left in the cold about the operation too long. I should have guessed!"

"We can't worry about that now," Carter said, throwing off the covers and sliding his feet to the floor. "Christ, I'm naked!"

"The doctor had to put fourteen stitches in your side," Weatherby said. "Whaddaya expect? You're a patient."

"No more," Carter growled. "Give me some shorts."

"But the wound might open. You—" Tamara protested.

"And my pants. We've got to get to the Lido. What time is it?"

"A little past four. What do you think—"

Weatherby's question was interrupted by the sharp double ring of the phone.

"Yeah, Weatherby here . . . oh, shit."

Carter paused, his pants half up and half down. Tamara's eyes were intent on Weatherby's suddenly contorted face as he spoke again.

"Get him out of there. Cover it up, but not before you do a complete cleanup. I'll get back to you!"

He slammed the phone down and turned to face them.

"Koenigburger?" Carter asked.

"No," Weatherby replied, his eyes on the woman. "Evidently you were compromised. They've already started the cleanup."

"I don't understand," she said.

"It's Norman Ahrens. My man found him about five minutes ago, hanging from the chandelier in his hotel room."

"They tried to make it look like suicide," Carter said.

"Yeah, but we found him first and we know different."

"Let's get to the Lido," Carter said. "Tamara, stay in this apartment, don't go through the panel back to your own. They may still try for you tonight."

"No, this is my fault. I'm going."

"Suit yourself, but let's move!"

Everything was going smoothly, like a calm sea with no wind.

The concierge and the two women in the office were securely bound and out of the way. The four night maids and the night porter were occupying their respective cubicles in the same condition. Alain Mittain and his men had taken the two night janitors and the watchmen. They were bound, gagged, and locked in a basement storage room.

It had taken Pierre Donet four minutes flat to open both the large and the small safes. Dino Foche had his laser drill and other equipment ready when the door to the safe-deposit boxes opened before him.

That had been fifteen minutes before, and Dino had already opened thirty-two of the boxes. Their lids barely fell away before Marta and Donet were stuffing the contents into special canvas bags.

So far, there had been no interruptions. Carmine Fragunet, in his doorman's uniform, had been forced to take no one trying to come in the Place Vendôme entrance. Claudia Biget was holding up well on the switchboard. Thus far, she had handled the two incoming and the single outgoing calls without a tremor in her voice.

Julian Carmont manned the desk himself, still in his white jump suit, but with the hood pulled down.

It was a calculated risk. He wore dark glasses, and had added flesh and whiskers to his face from a makeup kit. The figuring was that he could, if confronted by any early departing guest, pose as a computer maintenance man working on the hotel's equipment.

The two-way in his hand crackled, and Alain Mittain's voice came over it from somewhere in the bowels of the hotel.

"Alain here . . ."

"Go ahead."

"I have the master keys to all the VIP suites. We're starting through them now."

"Excellent. There are sixteen full, six vacant," Carmont replied, and he read off the names of the vacant suites to save the crew time.

"Got them. We're off."

"Alain?"

"Yes?"

"Hurry it, even if you have to leave one or two. The morning breakfast crew comes in at five sharp. We have to be out by four-fifty."

"Will do."

"Julian . . ."

It was Marta at his elbow. "Yes?"

"We're separating, like you said, cash and negotiable securities in one set of bags, jewels in another. What about this?"

She held up a velvet-lined box. Inside it was an ivory icon of the Mother and Child, covered with gold and encrusted with gems.

"It might have ransom value over and above the gems. Put it in the bag of fencibles."

She nodded and hurried off.

The sharp click of women's heels approaching from the hall made him turn back to face the reception area. Beneath the desk, he slipped the safety on his pistol to "off" as two garishly dressed girls—one with green hair, one with purple—came around the corner of the lobby.

Both of the women, Nanette and Babette, had memorized every word coming out of Almar Koenigburger's mouth. It had become increasingly difficult to understand some of what he said because his body had twice erupted in convulsions. After the second one, he seemed to be fighting off the effects of the drug.

"He has the constitution of an ox. I gave him more than enough."

"Give him another shot!"

"Do you think we should?"

"We'll have to. The Madonna is in the safe-deposit boxes. You can't get into them until five. One of us will clean up and walk him down to the desk."

"Pose as his daughter?"

"Yes, that will do. Hurry!"

Babette gave Koenigburger another shot, and they continued the interrogation.

Weatherby, flanked by two dark-suited agents on his right and two more on his left, exited the Lido, turned right, and hurried along the Champs-Élysées.

In the second of two cars, Carter saw them coming. He opened the door and painfully pulled himself upright to stand on the curb.

There was little traffic, and their heels made ominous sounds on the sidewalk. The lights from the Arc de Triomphe over Carter's shoulder danced across the men, illuminating their faces as they rushed forward.

Carter didn't like the expressions he saw.

"You took long enough."

Weatherby shrugged. "It's a big place, seats twelve hundred. And even at this hour there are a lot of straggling drinkers after the last show."

"But no Koenigburger."

Weatherby shook his head. "And no punk whores. We checked everywhere and everyone. Finally got the waiter who handled that section, claims he remembers the two women with the crazy hair."

"And . . ."

"Says they picked up on two American types and left with them."

"What about Koenigburger?"

"None of the waiters remembers him, but then some of them have already left for the night."

"Damn." Carter breathed, slapping the side of the sedan. "I could swear they were going after Koenigburger. What time is it?"

Weatherby checked his watch. "Almost five."

"Okay, let's blanket the Ritz. We'll take him when he comes down and heads for the apartment."

"Think that's wise?"

"I think," Carter said, "it's all we've got left. Tamara's cold, we know that. By now they might know that *she* knows she is."

"It's still a better chance to let the German go for the apartment and hope," Weatherby said. "They won't take him on the street."

"True."

"And besides, it's a good chance that this Madonna icon is in the hotel safe-deposit boxes. It will take Koenigburger himself to get it out."

Carter nodded and peered at the other man for several seconds through the smoke.

"Okay, but we still cover the Ritz."

Seconds later, the two cars had made a U-turn on the Champs-Élysées and were slowly heading for the Place Vendôme less than twenty blocks away.

In the distance, they could hear the sharp, distinctive wail of police sirens.

They thought nothing of it.

Paris was a big city. There was a lot of crime.

"What's the matter with him?"

Almar Koenigburger's face, within minutes of the last shot, had turned a deep crimson. Now it was deathly pale and he was gasping for air.

"What is it?"

"I don't know. He can't seem to get his breath."

"Well, work on him. You take the chest. I'll give him respiration."

Together, the two women worked over the aging German's heaving body. Now and then his legs would twitch and his arms would flail the air. But the raspy, hoarse chokes continued.

"His pulse is erratic."

"Work harder!"

They did, but to no avail. Minutes later, Koenigburger gasped a last time and the body was still.

The green-haired one lifted her lips from his and looked into her comrade's wide eyes.

"What is it?"

"I think he's dead."

Quickly the pulse was felt for at wrist and throat.

"*Merde, merde, merde!*"

"Wait, it's all right. We can do it ourselves."

"What?"

"You've got the gun in your purse?"

"Yes."

"And we have his key. The concierge has the master key. We'll make the concierge open the safe-deposit box for us. There will be no one around the desk at this hour, and he will never be able to describe us looking like this."

"You're right. Hurry, leave him!"

Alain Mittain opened the last VIP suite on his list as furtively as he had opened the others.

Thus far, the loot in jewels and cash had been fantastic. It was amazing how many people didn't bother to put their valuables in the hotel safe-deposit boxes.

But then, this was the Ritz. Where could you be safe in Paris if not at the Ritz?

The sitting room was empty. Mittain motioned his partner to check the bedroom on the right. The man held up the pad of chloroform in his hand and moved away while Mittain took the bedroom to the left.

It was empty. The bed had not been slept in.

"Alain . . . Alain!"

"What is it?"

"Come here, quickly!"

Mittain rushed into the other bedroom. The bed was a mess. On it was a bloated, half-naked man, his skin fish-belly white. His eyes were open, vacant and staring.

Mittain had seen many men like this.

"He's dead."

"How do you know?"

"I know, that's all. He's dead. Go through his clothes. I'll check the briefcase."

They worked quickly.

"Nothing but a few bills and change in the clothes."

"Not so the briefcase," Mittain replied, waving stacks of francs, marks, and dollars. "Another one who didn't trust the safe-deposit boxes. Let's go!"

As they passed the bed, Alain Mittain saluted the corpse.

"Au revoir, monsieur. Merci."

"Bonjour, mesdemoiselles," Julian Carmont said as the two women reached the counter. "You are up early."

He was about to bring his gun up, when the green-haired one's hands came above the desk. In them, and very steady, she held a pistol of her own.

Carmont froze.

"You are obviously a maintenance person. Where is the concierge?"

Over the woman's shoulder, Carmont saw Mittain and his man appear around the corner. His gaze didn't falter, and he slowly raised his left hand, keeping the right holding his own gun, under the counter.

Alain Mittain was a good man. Carmont knew the situation could be handled.

"I am afraid he is on one of the floors, *mademoiselle*, a disturbance. What is it you want?"

"We have a key," said Purple Hair. "We want no more than to get into one safe-deposit box."

"Who has the master key?" asked the other one.

"I'm afraid . . ."

That was all Carmont got out of his mouth.

Mittain took the one with the gun in quick, smooth movements: a chop across the wrist and a second one across the back of the neck.

Green Hair went down in a heap, but Purple Hair dived for the gun. Mittain's helper was on her in a flash.

But to all three men's surprise, the woman was a wildcat. Not only that, she was a trained wildcat.

She came up from her stance without the gun but fighting like hell. Her elbow caught him in the crotch, and the top of her head hailed him soundly on the point of the chin.

He went back and down, arms out, hitting the marble floor with his spine and head.

Alain Mittain went for her but got nearly the same treatment. The heel of a hand caught his chin, sending his head back and exposing the column of his throat.

Her other arm was cocked for a death-dealing blow, when Carmont leaned far over the counter and cracked the long barrel of his pistol on the back of her head.

She staggered but refused to fall.

Mittain, ever a man with his wits about him, caught her square on the point of the chin with an uppercut.

Finally she folded to the floor, still not completely out, but down.

"Mon Dieu, what was that all about?" Mittain rasped.

"They wanted into one of the safe-deposit boxes, and they were willing to use the gun to get at it. I could see it in that one's eyes."

Mittain chuckled. "Robbers robbing the robbers? I don't get it."

"Don't bother to try, we haven't time. Get them tied up. Put them with the others!" Carmont headed for the adjoining room.

Pierre Donet met him at the door. "Trouble?"

"A little. We took care of it. How many boxes to go?"

"Six."

"Hurry it up, we only have ten minutes."

"Home base . . . home base!" barked the walkie-talkie on Carmont's belt.

He lifted it to his face and barked into it. "Go ahead, Carmine."

"The garbage truck is three blocks away, on rue St.-Honoré!"

"No problem," Carmont replied. "Jam the door and bring the limo around to the Cambon exit."

"Check!"

Julian Carmont was smiling as he replaced the walkie-talkie on his belt.

They would make it, with minutes to spare.

EIGHT

Every move was prompt to the second. They all congregated at the service entrance door. The white jump suits and gloves were stripped off and, added to the hardware, placed in a third canvas bag.

On the loading dock, the bags were stuffed into garbage cans.

"All right," Carmont said, jumping from the dock and opening the door of the limousine, "you all know what to do for the next two days. We meet in Honfleur on Sunday!"

Without a word, they dispersed.

Carmont, Marta Penn, and Dino Foche got into the back of the limousine. The door had barely closed behind them before Carmine Fragunet, the doorman's uniform discarded now, shot the big Mercedes forward.

Pierre Donet and Caludia Biget, dressed in evening clothes and looking like two elegant Parisians ending a long night on the town, walked toward the Place de l'Opéra.

On rue Scribe, they turned into the Grand Hôtel.

The day doorman was just unlocking the door.

"*Bonjour, monsieur, madame.*"

"*Bonjour.*"

"A beautiful morning."

"*Oui, monsieur,*" Donet replied with a wide smile, "a fitting end to a beautiful night in Paris."

They took the elevator to the third floor and entered the suite they would occupy for the next two days as a honeymooning couple from Trouville, in Normandy.

Alain Mittain and his partner walked quickly to the Seine via the Place de la Concorde. At the edge of the bridge, they descended stone steps to the river and a speedboat.

Seconds later, they were heading east toward Boulogne-Billancourt.

Their part of the operation was not yet done.

At the Pont d'Issy, they would tie up and abandon the stolen boat. Then they would walk two long blocks to an alley off the rue de Vanves, where a stolen Citroën with Luxembourg plates awaited them.

From there it was a fifteen-minute drive to an underpass, about a mile short of the Passendoor garbage incinerator.

"Nanette" and "Babette" were, respectively, Eva Stalnik and Sofia Dobroskov. They had been trained by the KGB since their early teens in French culture, language, and geography.

By the time of the Madonna affair, they had been operating undercover in and around Paris for nearly five years.

The thin nylon line that had been tied to their wrists and ankles was child's play. Through muscle expansion and contraction, it was a simple feat to loosen their bonds.

But, wisely, neither of them did it until the thieves were gone.

Their training had been excellent. They could kill ruthlessly in the blink of an eye. But odds of eight-to-two were too great even for them with their training in hand-to-hand combat, especially when over half of the eight were armed.

The voluptuous Eva was the first to release herself. She ripped the tape from her mouth and did the same for Sofia Dobroskov.

"Did you hear the little one with the drill?" she whispered.

"Yes. He called himself the new Prince of Eure."

"And the tall one with the low voice mentioned Deauville."

"At least it's a lead." Sofia nodded. "Let's go!"

Across the room, Charles Portain kicked his feet against the floor and mumbled wildly behind his gag.

"Leave them," Eva said, stomping her own feet to get circulation back into her legs. "We don't have time to answer questions."

Sofia nodded. "And they will wonder what we are doing here without being guests at the hotel."

Together they raced down the long arcade toward the rue Cambon exit.

"It's locked!"

Furiously they returned to the arcade, intending to sprint back toward the main entrance at Place Vendôme.

"Look!" Sofia Dobroskov exclaimed.

Her bejeweled fingers pointed toward a painted door near the dining room marked in French, Service: Staff Only.

As one, they bolted through the door and down two flights of steel steps that ended in a long hallway.

"This way. It leads to a service exit!"

They were only a few steps short of the outside door, when it suddenly opened.

A thin, sallow-faced man with tired, hooded eyes and a drooping black mustache momentarily filled the exit. He scarcely managed to curse and jump to the side as the two women rushed forward.

Barely pausing, they took the steps of the loading dock three at a time and darted left at rue Cambon. At the corner they darted right and practically dove into the rear seat of a Renault sedan.

"What took you so damned long?" Maurice Petrade hissed, throwing the car into gear and lurching away from the curb. "I've been waiting half the night!"

"We'll explain later," Eva replied.

"Yes," Sophia grunted. "Now get us to the flat so we can

wash our hair and get out of these clothes.''

"The flat was raided. Nadia and Leonid are dead. I saw them carry the bodies out.''

"*Merde!*" Eva Stalnik cried. "Who?''

"Americans, I think. I've already called emergency. I am to take you to the château in Cluny. Did you get the Madonna?''

"No.''

"You *didn't*?'' he growled, lifting his eyes to the rearview mirror and almost running into a slow-moving taxi. "Then where is it?''

"Only a guess,'' Sophia replied through thin lips, "but we think it's headed for Normandy.''

Emilio Roderigo Tettrini watched the two weird-looking women until they were out of sight, and then chuckled to himself.

Probably a couple of whores, he thought, with hotel security right behind them.

But as he headed up the stairs and down the arcade toward the registration desk, he didn't see security. In fact, he didn't see anyone.

As he had every morning, six days a week for the last two years, Emilio tapped the call bells for Charles Portain.

Portain would emerge from behind the key and mail racks, give the little Italian immigrant a condescending stare, and toss him the keys to the kitchen.

But this morning was different. There was no Charles Portain, and the area behind the desk was silent. Usually by this hour it was humming with activity in preparation for the shift change.

And then he heard it, a muffled voice quickly followed by an odd thumping sound, as if someone were pounding on the parquet floor.

"Monsieur Portain, it is I, Emilio! The keys, *si'l vous plaît*. I must open the kitchen!''

More pounding, louder now.

Curiously, Emilio went around the counter and peeked his head around the partition. "Monsieur Por . . . *mon Dieu!*"

Charles Portain and the two men were tied up on the floor. The night concierge's eyes were wide with appeal, and sweat poured off his face.

Gingerly, Emilio stepped forward and removed the tape from Portain's lips.

"What has happened, *monsieur?*"

"Untie me quickly, you fool!" Portain screamed in a very uncharacteristic falsetto voice. "There has been a robbery!"

"A robbery? *Mon Dieu, monsieur!* You have been robbed?"

"No, you cretin, the Ritz has been robbed! Untie me!"

Emilio Tettrini remembered the two running women in the outlandish clothes and "new wave" hair as he attacked Charles Portain's bonds.

He wondered if the hotel would elevate his station and give him a raise when he told the police that he could describe the robbers perfectly.

The south entrance to the Place Vendôme was blocked off by two police vehicles. Above them, Carter could see that the north entrance was the same.

Around the entrance to the Ritz, plainclothes and uniformed officers were milling like bees around the hive.

The two sedans rocked to a halt, but no one moved, waiting for some command from either Carter or Weatherby.

"What the hell is this?" Carter exclaimed.

Weatherby whistled. "It's big," he said, eyeing the scene, "whatever it is."

"Any of you got an in with the local gendarmes?" Carter asked.

"I do, sir, with an Inspector Foulet," replied the agent beside Weatherby in the front seat.

"Well, see if you can get in there and find out what the hell this is all about. Use your diplomatic card. Tell them it's official. You have to see the officer in charge."

"Right."

The young agent jumped from the car and jogged across rue St.-Honoré. He flashed his papers and was moved right on through. The men in the car watched his retreating back as he ran across the cobblestones of Place Vendôme. Just as he disappeared into the Ritz entrance, Carter and Weatherby exchanged looks.

"Think it's our business?"

"Hard to say," Carter replied, sighing and leaning back in the seat. "I wouldn't think so. They like to keep as quiet as we do with this sort of thing."

"Yeah," Weatherby said, "let's hope."

The wound in Carter's side was throbbing now like a trip-hammer. The pain had started again, and it was shooting up to his brain, making it increasingly difficult to think clearly.

"Bad?" Tamara said from the seat beside him, noticing his discomfort.

"Not good, but I'll last," he replied, slipping his hand under his jacket and gingerly touching the bandage through his shirt.

It felt warm and wet, telling him it was bleeding again.

It was twenty minutes before the agent returned. His face, as he crawled in beside Weatherby, was gray.

"Well?" Carter said.

"Robbery. They hit the VIP suites, the hotel safes, and all the safe-deposit boxes. Got away clean."

"Any details?" Carter asked, his voice tight.

"A very pro job, fast and efficient. There were six or eight of them. The two women from the Hungarian apartment were involved, but I couldn't find out how."

Again Carter and Weatherby's eyes met. This time they held, and Weatherby spoke first, asking the question on both their minds.

"It would be a sure way to get the Madonna . . . Cover it up with a robbery."

"No," Tamara said. "I know them. They trained me, remember? The KGB is too cautious to try anything this risky."

"She's right," Carter said. "All they wanted to do was get the Madonna and get rid of Koenigburger. They could do that without going to all this trouble. What's that?"

An ambulance was just nosing out of the Place Vendôme. Through the glass, they could see that it was occupied, but the white-coated attendants in the rear were not working on the patient.

In fact, the patient was covered by a white sheet, face and all.

"One of the guests," the young agent in the front said. "Heart attack. The police don't think it's connected."

"Who is it?" Carter asked.

The agent shrugged, his face flushed. "I didn't get a name."

"Well, get your ass back in there and get one!" Carter cried, coming up in the seat and grimacing with the sudden pain the movement caused.

Again the man dived out of the car, this time with real speed. He made his trek and returned almost at once.

"I—I'm sorry, sir," he stammered.

"Who was it?"

"Our man, sir, Almar Koenigburger."

"Dammit! Weatherby . . ."

"Yeah."

"Use clout . . . a classified order, anything you need, go through the ministry if you have to. I want everything the locals have, including an itemization of the contents of the German's suite."

"Will do."

"In the meantime, get up to the safe house!"

The car surged forward, and Carter tried to make his mind work.

It wouldn't.

By the time they hit the outskirts of Paris, he had succumbed to the numbing pain and let sleep overtake him.

The stocky driver cursed halfway through the underpass and hit his air brakes. The big compactor truck ground to a halt inches from the rear bumper of the Citroën with the Luxembourg license plates.

The legs of two men extended from beneath the raised hood of the car.

"Hey, you're stopping traffic! Push that damned thing to the side or I'll do it for you!" the driver yelled.

Neither set of legs moved. The driver cursed again and called to his handler on the back of the truck.

"Émile . . . dammit, Émile!"

"What is it?" The man appeared in the passenger side window of the truck.

"Car trouble, I suppose. Give them a hand and push it to the curb."

Émile grunted and moved forward along the passenger side of the car. He had nearly reached the dangling legs, when the rest of the man's body and head appeared.

The head was encased in a ski mask, and a huge automatic pistol was in his hand.

"Stay calm, *monsieur*, and live to see the rest of the day."

The driver was too astonished to move as he watched the body on the driver's side emerge from beneath the hood. This man also wore a ski mask and held a huge automatic.

He held the gun steady in both hands as he walked back toward the truck. Its deadly muzzle was pointed right at the driver's face through the windshield.

"A garbage truck? . . . You want to steal a garbage truck?" he asked, amazed.

"Non, monsieur. We just want some of your garbage. Dump your load."

"Right here? In the street?"

"Dump it!" the man demanded, moving the gun until its

sight was painfully pushing into one of the driver's nostrils.

Automatically, his hands maneuvered the levers that commanded the hydraulic hoist.

With a groan, the truck's big compactor began to reverse. The second gunman ushered Émile into the cab and ran around the truck to open the rear doors.

Seconds later, garbage began to pour into the street.

"I have them!"

"Three?"

"Yes."

"The keys, *monsieur*."

The driver killed the engine and obligingly handed over the keys.

"*Merci, monsieur*," the man said with a nod and motioned to his comrade.

Open-mouthed, the driver watched the two masked men climb into the Citroën and drive away.

"Now, what the hell do you suppose that was all about?"

Beside him, Emile shrugged and then sighed. "Do we have to pick up all this shit?"

Twelve miles east of Paris, the Citroën turned north off the N13. Three miles later, it pulled into a narrow lane between two crumbling cement gate posts.

A few hundred yards up the lane, a small, ramshackle barn was nearly obscured by large oaks, poplars, and heavy shrubbery.

The Citroën halted beside the barn and both men jumped out. Without a word, one man dragged the three canvas sacks from the car while the other swung wide the doors.

Inside was a shiny new Simca van. Painted on its white side panel was MITTAIN AUTO PARTS, CAEN.

A shelf came down from the interior of the roof. The sacks were stored and the shelf was replaced.

"I'm hungry. Stop for breakfast at Pont-Audemer?"

"Why not?" Alain Mittain chuckled. "And a bottle of champagne! God knows we can afford it!"

NINE

The gentle hands on his shoulders awakened Carter but did not bring him to a state of ready alert. He found that impossible.

A doctor had rebandaged the wound, doped him, and ordered him to bed the moment they had reached the safe house.

Weatherby had promised to handle everything from the Paris end. As Carter fought the fog of sleep from his brain, he hoped the man had been able to do just that.

He realized that he had been sagging when the hands started shaking his shoulders again.

"Nick . . . Nick, can you wake up?"

It was Tamara. She had wound her glossy black hair into a long braid, tied it, and let it hang, Chinese style, over one shoulder. Somewhere between the time they arrived and now, she had changed into a baggy sweatshirt with U.C.L.A. across its front and a pair of jeans.

Carter managed a smile.

"What?" she said, lifting her hands from his shoulders and taking a step back.

"Nothing," he replied. "I was just thinking that now you look like the teen-ager that Ahrens described."

She laughed, and then, together, the smiles disappeared from their faces as they remembered that Norman Ahrens was dead.

"What time is it?"

"A little past one in the morning."

"Jesus, I've been out for thirteen hours?"

"Almost fourteen. Weatherby and his men are back. They are downstairs now."

Carter eased his feet to the floor and tested his equilibrium. With a groan he managed to stand, unaided, and then noticed that he was naked.

"This is getting to be a habit!"

"I've laid out a clean set of clothes, there, on the other bed." She smiled.

"You're getting to be quite a little mother."

"It's . . . well, it's at least something I can do well."

He looked up to see the sharp set of her jaw and the sadness in her eyes. She had gambled on trading something big for her freedom, and that something had slipped right through her fingers.

"Don't let it get to you, Tamara. Ahrens had already made all the arrangements for your disappearance. You won't be going back."

She averted her eyes. "I don't know what Weatherby has found out, but I would like you to promise me something."

"Within reason."

"If you find out where the Madonna is, and you go after it, I would like to go, too."

"I'll think about it . . . in return for something from you."

"Anything," she said, taking a step nearer.

"A cup of hot black coffee laced with brandy."

He moved toward the bath on wobbly legs, and her voice followed him. "I'll get it," she called, then chuckled lightly. "And, by the way, you don't need to bathe. I gave you a hospital bath while you were asleep."

He heard her slip from the room and concentrated on making himself whole again.

After dunking his head into cold water a few times, he ran the bowl with steaming hot and managed a shaky shave.

He was just finishing when Tamara reappeared with a cup and saucer.

"Half and half, brandy and coffee. All right?"

"Just as I like it," Carter sighed, gratefully taking the strong, rich brew from her outstretched hands. "Tell Weatherby I'll be down in ten minutes."

She nodded, and Carter attacked the staleness in his mouth with a toothbrush.

By the time he got into his underwear, a tan shirt, and a pair of rust-colored, lightweight trousers, he felt human again.

As he walked to the door, he noticed his Luger in its shoulder rig and Hugo in his spring-triggered chamois sheath neatly arranged on a chair by the bed.

Well, he thought, *now she knows a lot of my secrets. How many of hers do I know?*

Carter wolfed down a double appetizer of shrimp and tackled an entree of trout and potatoes as Weatherby ran through the intricacies of the Ritz robbery. He also read the highlights of the depositions taken from the hotel employees.

"Koenigburger's death was listed as a heart attack. It's confirmed, but they did find traces of the drug Soporocaine in his system."

"That can probably be attributed to the two women, the 'punk rockers,'" Carter added.

"Probably." Weatherby nodded. "It would appear that they did a number on him right from the beginning. They probably got the information they wanted, and then Koenigburger blanked."

"So they went down to the desk to clean out Koenigburger's safe-deposit box, and found out the place was already being robbed."

"It must have been that," Tamara said. "If they already had the Madonna, they wouldn't have tried what they did."

Carter pushed his plate away, poured coffee and brandy, and leaned back in his chair to light a cigarette.

"So it's a stalemate," he said, exhaling a cloud of smoke and furrowing his brow in concentration. "Tamara was to be used only as a backup, and perhaps not even that, since they hit Norman Ahrens just about the time the two women were working on Koenigburger."

The petite Russian woman nodded, her face flushing under Carter's intense gaze. "I cannot remember where, along the way, I compromised my position and that of Ahrens, but I must have. I am so sorry."

"It goes with the territory, Tamara," Carter said. "Something we all live with in the field."

Weatherby noisily rolled the ice in his glass. "I checked out the name 'Maurice' you remembered. Your guess was right, a waiter at the Lido. He was probably the one who gave us the wrong steer about the women leaving with two Americans."

"Where is he now?"

Weatherby shrugged. "Probably long gone. He didn't show up for work tonight. We checked the address he gave the club on his employment form. It was an empty room above a tailor's shop in Montparnasse."

"If it helps," Tamara offered, "I remember a few names from my days of filing in Moscow, before I was activated. There are several female agents here in Paris, but from the description of the hotel employees and your man who followed them to the Lido, I think I can guess who they are."

"That might help a lot down the line," Carter said.

"If they are anywhere in your computers, the names would be Eva Stalnik and Sofia Dobroskov."

Weatherby was hurriedly scribbling on a legal pad. "Do you know their cover names?"

"No."

He ripped the page off and handed it to one of the sub-agents, who scurried from the room. After rekindling the stub of a cigar between his teeth, he rolled his eyes back up to the Killmaster.

"What do you think?"

"I think that the Ritz hit was legit. It had nothing to do with Koenigburger. They were too thorough and did too many things. The chloroform on all the VIP guests, for instance, and the foul-up with the two female agents."

Weatherby puffed and nodded. "Agreed. Do you think the other side knows any more about where the loot went than we do?"

Carter shrugged. "It's a toss-up. Name of the game; if they don't, find out first."

"Think you can do that?"

"Maybe," Carter sighed, "maybe not. But it's worth a try. I've still got some old connections among the French lowlifes . . . and some who might know who has the class and expertise to pull off a job this size."

"But will they talk?"

"One might. She owes me a big one from a long time ago. Can you get me a small plane, a charter, first thing in the morning to Marseilles?"

"No problem."

"Nick . . ."

Tamara Petrovna had moved across the room to stand directly in front of Carter's chair.

"Yeah?"

"If you find out where the Madonna is, I want to help."

Carter shifted his gaze to Weatherby. The other man averted his eyes and made a big deal of extinguishing his cigar before speaking.

"No way."

"Why?" she asked, her voice raspy with demand.

"You're set up for further debriefing in Washington, and from there it's Switzerland and a new name."

"Then you trust me enough to honor my defection, but not enough to let me finish what I have started!"

"There isn't a hell of a lot you can do from here on," Carter said.

"I think there is," she insisted. "What if they know, as well, where the Madonna is? They will be going after it, and probably *you* at the same time."

"True."

"I know them by sight; you don't. You may need my eyes in the back of your head."

And, Carter thought, *you could also be the eyes in the back of their heads.*

She read his meaning. But instead of arguing further, she stood and, with iron in her spine, walked from the room.

"She might have a point, you know," Weatherby growled. "They have people in France that we don't have a thing on, and they can get others in on a moment's notice."

"I know," Carter said, his eyes burning the door that had just closed behind the petite woman. "I'll think on it. In the meantime, get me that plane, and have a car waiting in Marseilles."

"Right."

"And one other thing. Get Washington on the horn, all agencies."

"What do you need?"

"Everything they can give on a gypsy woman named Serena. She used to go for the highest bidder. I nailed her a few years ago, along with a few crazy Satan worshipers, in a place called Pastoria, in southern France."

"She owes you?"

"Yeah. I let her live after she tried to kill me."

"I'll get on it."

Weatherby left the room, and Carter made his way up the short flight of stairs to the bedroom he had been assigned.

As he descended toward sleep, an image of the tall, voluptuously beautiful Serena waved on the rear of his eyelids.

She was holding his own gun, with the muzzle pointed toward Carter's belly.

Carter was in the deep drowsy area, halfway between wakefulness and sound sleep, when he heard the sound. It was the soft scuff of slippered feet in the hall outside his room.

The feet paused. He could almost hear their owner's light breathing.

Then the unmistakable sound of the knob being turned drove all sleep from his mind. His body tensed and his hand slid under the pillow, the fingers closing around Hugo as he opened his eyes to slits.

Even in a safe house, the Killmaster's old habits of survival couldn't be discarded.

The door opened and closed swiftly, just enough to let her small body pass through.

The room's drapes were pulled, but moonlight still spilled through a slight break in their center. It was light enough for Carter to see her move toward the bed.

Tamara Petrovna had changed into an ankle-length, deep blue robe that clung tightly to her tiny waist and flared outward with the flow of her hips.

She was less than a yard from the side of the bed when she stopped. Carter's hand stopped tugging Hugo from beneath the pillow at the same time.

"Nick . . ."

"Yes."

"I knew you were awake. I could tell from your breathing."

"So what?"

"Move over."

Her hands worked at the belt of the robe, and it fell away.

She was nude beneath it, the aureoles of her small, pert breasts darkly brilliant against the alabaster lightness of her skin.

There was a smooth movement, and he felt the warmth of her body caress his. She moved closer, and the clean scent of her hair invaded his nostrils.

"In Marseilles, you will find someone who knows someone who will know who committed the robbery?"

"I think so."

"And then you will know where to look for the Madonna?"

"I hope so."

"But you won't take me with you."

"I'm thinking about it."

"How bad does your wound hurt you?"

"Not much."

She laughed and moved her head until the light fell across her face. The sight and scent and feel of her had his body already tingling with awareness.

She had pinned her long black hair in a twist at the back of her head. When she smiled and narrowed her lustrous almond eyes, the habitual look of innocence disappeared. In its place was the look of a lusty woman.

"Not enough to make this uncomfortable?"

She molded the bottom half of her body to his and lifted one of his hands to her breast.

"Not uncomfortable at all," he growled.

"I am small."

"You're just right."

He held the breast, squeezed and taunted it a little. The nipple became pebble-hard in his palm.

She sighed faintly and slipped one of her marvelously smooth legs between his knees as her lips reached his.

Their lips met, and then their tongues.

For a long moment they embraced that way. Then Carter's hand began to glide lower on her body. Down it went, to her gently rounded belly, to lightly creep over her hips to the full thrust of her buttocks.

His fingers dug into the firm flesh. She stirred against him, further heightening his desire with the softness of her sex as his hand moved up her back.

And then Tamara's hands were on him, returning the intimate caresses, awakening him as he was awakening her. Not that it was necessary. Their bodies were ready, their reflexes perfectly attuned. By this time no preamble was necessary.

What is unnecessary, however, is sometimes still desirable. They enjoyed what they were doing, so the acts that with some couples were a matter of grim, harsh, tension-producing necessity became acts of fun with them.

Fingertips wandered over welcoming skin. Lips toyed playfully. Breasts and thighs gave themselves up to the gentle, loving caresses of the prelude.

Then it was time.

They both knew it, innately, automatically. No word was spoken. They simply turned toward one another, and she arched her body, and he gently, gently slipped into the harbor of her love.

The moment after their bodies had joined, neither of them moved. They remained motionless, eyes open in the darkness, smiling at one another. Carter bent his head down, lightly kissed her lips. She answered with a playful inward quiver.

Then they began to move as passion surged in them.

There were no surprises, no unexpected deadfalls or traps. The curve of their lovemaking was a firm, soaring arc, up, up, up still higher, and they hovered for a moment, lips to lips, bodies joined from mouth to ankles, two human beings as close to one another as two human beings can ever get. And after that moment of calm hesitation came the breaking of the storm, the sudden thunderclap and the bright flash of lightning.

Their bodies moved and thrust in sudden urgency.

High, higher, highest.

The moment came.

Wave after shuddering wave of it, bodies merging and meshing, both attaining the peak of emotion in the same fraction of a fraction of a second, a perfect mating.

The double burst of pleasure came.

Then the slow, gentle retreat from the summit.

Carter brought her down as easily and as skillfully as he had brought her up. Soon they were lying side by side in the darkness, relaxed, drained of tensions, each comfortably aware of the other's warmth, of the other's nearness.

After a while Carter withdrew from her. He reached out, found the nearest swelling breast, and held it fondly for a moment. Tamara's fingers traced the line of his jaw lightly.

"Aside from how it may appear," she whispered, "I did that because I wanted to, not to convince you to take me along."

"I believe you."

The room was silent, with only the steady sound of their breathing disturbing the stillness.

"I have an idea," she finally said, "that might give us a lead if you are not successful in Marseilles."

"I'll listen," Carter replied.

"Allow Yuri Androssov to escape. He knows how to contact his people. If he is followed, we will know where he is headed."

Carter rolled his face toward her, with the barest suggestion of a smile curling his lips.

"That's a good suggestion, except it's already been done."

"What?"

"About an hour ago."

Without another word, Tamara slipped from the bed and slid the robe around her. "Perhaps one day I shall see you again, in Switzerland."

"Tamara . . ."

She stopped at the door but didn't turn. "Yes?"

"You'll stay here. I'll contact Weatherby from Marseilles and tell him where to have you meet me."

There was silence, and then a softly whispered, ''Thank you.''

For a moment Carter thought she was going to return to the bed.

She didn't.

Instead, she slipped from the room and quietly closed the door behind her.

That's good, Carter thought with satisfaction. She had separated business from pleasure.

TEN

It was almost noon by the time Carter parked the car on the high road above the old Marseilles harbor.

He had changed at the airport into a seaman's sweater and cap, and a pair of worse-for-wear blue dungarees. From the trunk he hoisted a worn duffel bag to his shoulder and walked down the hill toward the old quay.

Before him, the red-roofed old buildings, darkened by years of exposure to auto fumes, stretched to the bay and the sea beyond. Far out in the gray-brown haze, several pale ghosts of ships waited their turn to dock and begin the landing process.

As he walked, Carter went over in his mind the brief report on Serena he had received that morning.

The early stuff, before Carter had first met her, he already knew. She had been born Serafina Gamboli, in a little village south of Rome. Her father was a playboy aristocrat who had never married her mother, a sometime whore named Maria Gamboli.

She had followed in her mother's footsteps for a time in her early years but quickly found other, more profitable, uses for her beauty.

She also discovered that she had a much quicker mind than her sisters. She still used her body but gleaned information instead of coin. The coin came from selling the information to the highest bidder.

When Carter met her, she had accepted the KGB as highest bidder for both her active service and the information she could supply.

Why he had once let her go was academic, but he had.

Now he was glad, because the final part of the report was just about what he had expected.

Serena had stayed away from politics and turned her talents to good old-fashioned crime. Smuggling, fencing stolen goods, and running some big-time illegal card games all through Europe had become her forte.

According to Interpol, she was also suspected of financing and masterminding some very large heists in England and on the Continent.

Suspected, but never arrested or indicted.

For the past year, Serena had been quiet and dropped out of sight, maybe retired.

But retired or not, Carter guessed that Serena still kept in touch and had her fingers in lots of pies. If anyone could point him in the right direction, she could.

If he could find her.

At the moment, Interpol and the *Sûreté*—the French Criminal Investigation Department—wanted her very badly for questioning about some missing Exocet missiles that had turned up in some odd Third World countries.

He checked into the sleaziest hotel he could find and started making the rounds of Marseilles's waterfront dives, from the only half-bad fishermen's bars to the down-and-dirty underworld hangouts.

Casually, he mentioned his desire to find Serena, the gypsy, in four places, with little or no reaction or result.

In a fifth, he got some reaction.

It was a place called the Mariner's Hub, just off the quay, in an alley that hadn't seen a street cleaner since the end of the war.

Carter sensed pay dirt the moment he walked into the

place. It was a long, narrow room with smoke-darkened walls and the smell of stale beer and ages of perspiration.

On the left were nine or ten booths, with the bar set in the middle of the right wall. At the back, two doors indicated the men's and women's w.c.

Only two of the booths were occupied, one with a scar-faced giant in fisherman's clothes and a healthy redhead who looked forty but was probably in her teens when all the paint was washed off her face. The second booth was taken up by two dapper and surly *mecs* who were killing time until the night and their girls could be put to work.

There were two other fisherman-types at the bar, and a lone woman.

Carter bypassed the booths and took a stool at the bar.

"Monsieur?" The barman was fat, with a face that had collapsed into drooping flesh and two eyes that never stopped blinking.

"Whiskey . . . neat," Carter told the barman, not trying to hide his American-accented English.

He paid for his drink and was about to sip it, when the woman, two stools down, spoke to him.

"Americain, monsieur?"

Carter nodded and took her in with one quick glance. Near forty, blond, thin, with a faded blue sweater stretched over two large, sharp-ended funnels. Carter couldn't help thinking that under the sweater the funnels were empty.

"Would *monsieur* buy Claudette a drink?"

"Why not?"

The barman was quick. The lady drank gin, by the glass. A third of the gin disappeared, and she moved down to the stool beside his.

"I have not seen you before, *chéri*."

"Just came off my ship. I'm looking for someone, a gypsy woman."

She didn't take the bait, but Carter thought he saw the barman's ears twitch.

"You are a very attractive man."

"Thanks," Carter said, forcing a smile and toasting her with his glass. "Here's how."

"*Oui*, here's how," she replied, lifting her own glass.

The gin disappeared down the trapdoor of her throat. She set the glass on the bar and smiled. The smile meant only one thing.

Carter motioned to the fat man, and the glass was refilled. She clutched it and leaned her face close to his.

"If it is a woman you are looking for, *monsieur*, you needn't look any further."

"I'm looking for a special woman."

"My hotel room is very near. For two hundred francs, I will show you how special I can be."

Carter took two bills from his breast pocket, folded them around two of his fingers, and rested his hand on the bar.

"It would be worth double if I could find the gypsy woman, Serena."

The conversation stilled in the booths behind him. The barman fastened his pig eyes on Carter and backed through a door. The woman on the next stool nearly spilled her gin.

"You know Serena?" Carter asked, fixing her eyes with his.

"*Non, monsieur*. I know no one by that name."

Carter shrugged, picking his change up from the bar. "Too bad. I'm an old friend. I know she would want to see me."

He moved down the bar into the men's room. By the time he finished relieving himself, his eyes were watering and he was holding his nose.

Back at the bar, the old blonde's stool was empty. The fat barman was vigorously wiping the table between the big fisherman and the teen-ager with the thirtyish face.

Carter passed them and blinked his way into the sunlight. He turned right, crossed the street, and walked three blocks, checking over his shoulder all the way.

The old blonde was trailing him, but not closing the distance.

He hit two more bars, got some of the same guarded reaction he had received in the Mariner's Hub, but no takers.

The blonde was still tracking from a distance as he moved again, this time to a joint called the Cockroach.

It lived up to its name.

"Whiskey."

Carter was smelling the cheap contents of the glass when she came through the door . . . not the blonde, but the red-haired, heavily made-up teen-ager.

She smiled, and Carter smiled back. It looked like a beeline to him, but at the last minute she faded and slid her rear onto a stool two down from his.

She ordered a draft beer. The barman called her Hilary, but didn't seem to know her too well in spite of the first name.

Carter broke the ice. "What happened to your friend?"

"Friend . . ?"

"The big guy with the scar and the rubber boots . . . the fisherman."

She shrugged. "He probably went fishing. Besides"—she paused and spun on the stool to face him directly—"you look more prosperous."

"Do I, now?"

"I thought maybe I could do better than Claudette."

"Claudette . . . ?"

"The old hag you were talking to in the Hub."

"Maybe you can."

She closed the distance, and ran her hand up and down the inside of his thigh for the benefit of anyone watching. "For a thousand francs, I might know the name of someone who knows the gypsy woman."

"A thousand francs is a lot of money for a name."

She shrugged but managed a wan smile. "A thousand francs is not much compensation for two broken arms."

"I see. Then the gypsy woman doesn't want to be found? Not even by a friend?"

"That I do not know. I know a man. His name is Pepe. I

will take you to him. What he tells you . . ."

The words trailed off, and again the small, frail shoulders lifted in a shrug.

"Okay. Shall we go?"

"Certainly, as soon as you give me a thousand francs."

They walked for nearly twenty minutes, around the quay and along the narrow canals leading inland from the harbor.

Carter stayed close to her, ready to put the arm on her if she bolted. Either she was legit, or she was out to con him for a thousand. The francs he wouldn't mind losing, but he didn't want to waste a lot of time going through the bar routine again.

"There."

Carter followed her pointing finger to a short, narrow barge bobbing in the canal.

"You're not coming on board?"

"No. His name is Pepe. Give me the other half of the thousand-franc note."

"Not until I come back."

She tossed him another French shrug, sat on a tie-up post, and lit a cigarette.

Carter jumped to the deck of the barge and moved aft to the hatch that led belowdecks. It was closed. He knocked, waited, and knocked again.

"*Oui*?"

"Pepe?"

"*Oui* . . ."

The hatch burst open, and before Carter could spring back, two hamlike hands had filled themselves with the front of his sweater. He was yanked from his feet, whirled, and thrown completely across the cabin against the far bulkhead.

He didn't slide clear to the deck, but almost.

"Are you police, *monsieur*? . . . *Sûreté*? . . . Interpol?"

The Killmaster gasped some air back into his lungs and shook his head to clear it. When his eyes focused, he saw the scar-faced fisherman looming above him, fists knotted, ready.

"No, I am an American."

"American police?"

"No. You know Serena?"

"I know the gypsy woman. She is a friend. That is why Pepe wants to know who you are."

"My name is Carter. If you can contact her, just tell her that Carter must see her."

"What about?"

"I can only tell her that myself."

"No, you must tell Pepe."

"I can't do that," Carter replied, using his heels on the deck to push himself upright.

"Then Pepe will have to beat the shit out of you."

He rushed, head pulled into his shoulders, both forearms up, fists only inches apart. Carter relaxed and took the surge like a wrestler, turning his body to the side at the last second.

The left was already jabbing. Carter caught the wrist with his left hand and threw his right shoulder into the man's face.

Pepe stumbled and both of them went down, making kindling of a table in the process.

The guy was big, and probably an experienced barroom fighter. Carter had Hugo, but he didn't want to go that far. Once the stiletto came into the open, the Killmaster knew he would probably have to use it.

He wanted Pepe alive.

Pepe, his left wrist still locked in Carter's left hand, tried a high, wild right to the Killmaster's jaw. Carter rolled and nailed the scarred face again with his shoulder.

This time, the connection was solid. Bone and cartilage gave, and blood squirted like a geyser from the big man's nose and lips.

Carter was about to bring a knee into action, when Pepe got his left arm free. At the same time, he used his superior weight to roll up over the Killmaster.

A left rocked the side of Carter's jaw. He saw bloodred

stars, then the right coming straight down as a follow-up.

He rolled his head to the side, felt the fist rake his ear, and then heard an agonizing scream of pain from the man above him.

Pepe had smashed his fist into the hardwood deck by Carter's head. At least three—and probably all—of his knuckles were broken.

He didn't know it, but it was the blow that lost him the fight.

Carter slipped him easily, but Pepe came up off the deck after him, his smashed right hand hanging uselessly at his side.

He tried a left.

Carter caught the wrist and elbow, and brought the forearm down hard on his knee. Bones cracked like a rifle shot in the cabin, and Pepe screamed again.

Carter let the arm go and followed the man as he staggered away.

"Last chance, Pepe. I'm legit. I want to meet with Serena."

Pepe answered with his right foot, bringing it up in a kick to Carter's groin. Another sidestep, and Carter, using the man's own leg, drove him into the bulkhead.

A left, a right, and then a flurry with both fists at once into the midsection. When Pepe was all out of air, Carter stepped back and kneecapped his right leg with a well-aimed kick.

Pepe had barely dropped to his left knee on the deck before Carter went to work on his face.

When he was sure the big Frenchman was out, he stepped back and let him thud to the deck.

The girl's eyes opened in surprise when Carter pulled himself to the dock and approached her. She stood, but she didn't run, and by the time he reached her, the surprise was gone, replaced by calm appraisal.

"Pepe?"

"Hurting very bad. He'll need a hospital for a few days."

"You are very tough, *monsieur*."

"Very," Carter replied, ripping the small black bag from her hands.

In her wallet he found an identity card and a driver's license.

"Hilary St. Pierre," he read aloud. "Rue du Refuge."

He dropped his half of the thousand-franc note in the bag, joined it with another, and handed the bag back to her.

"My name is really Carter. I'm in room twelve, the Albacore. You know it?"

"I know it."

"If you don't come for me by seven o'clock tonight with information about how to reach the gypsy woman, Hilary, I'll come looking for you."

He moved around her and lit a cigarette as he walked away without looking back.

It was five minutes to seven when Carter heard a soft rap on his door. He rolled off the bed and, in the same movement, filled his hand with Wilhelmina.

"*Oui?*"

"Monsieur Carter?"

"*Oui.*"

"Would you open the door, please?"

"Are you standing on the opposite side of the hall?"

"*Oui, monsieur.*"

"You'd better be."

He dropped the chain and opened the door, the Luger up and ready.

The man was tall, lean, and calm, his eyes barely taking notice of the gun. He was dressed in a black suit, with black driving gloves and a beret.

"I am Eugene, *monsieur*, driver for Monsieur Roland. I have instructions to take you to the villa."

Carter smiled. He had never met Roland DuPree, but he knew about him. Everybody in France knew Monsieur Roland DuPree, the fixer.

● ● ●

The villa was a three-story affair on spacious grounds in the hills above St.-Tronc. It was the kind of neighborhood where even the servants drove expensive Citroëns.

The masters didn't drive. They were chauffeured everywhere in Rolls-Royces.

A butler opened the front door before Carter reached it.

"Good evening, *monsieur*. If you will follow me, please."

He had barely glanced at Carter's common clothing, and his eyes hadn't made any comment. His boss saw all kinds.

The room was comfortable, almost cozy, even though it was forty feet long and nearly as wide. Heavy velvet draperies were drawn across floor-to-ceiling windows at one end, and a black stone fireplace took up the entire wall at the other end.

In between were antiques . . . nothing later than Louis XVI.

The butler led him to the fireplace, where a phony log burned brightly and two comfortable club chairs were arranged beside a bar table. On the tray rested Waterford crystal, a dozen bottles, a siphon, and a solid gold ice bucket. In the center of all this was a dish of canapés that would have fed a dozen very hungry people.

"Monsieur Roland will be with you shortly."

"Thank you."

"Would you care for a cocktail?"

"I'll help myself."

"As you wish, *monsieur*." The butler floated out.

Carter poured a large whiskey, hit it once with the siphon bottle, and folded into a chair.

Five minutes later a panel in the wall to his right swished open, and Roland DuPree walked into the room. He was a dapper man, slightly above middle height, and dressed in a black silk smoking jacket with a bloodred shawl collar.

He stopped in front of Carter's chair, peered down at him over half-glasses, and smiled.

"Monsieur Carter."

The Killmaster didn't rise until the other man had offered his hand. When he did, Carter rose and pumped it once.

"Monsieur Roland. We've never met, but I feel I know you by reputation."

The smile in reply was more like a satisfied leer. He spoke as he fixed himself a drink and took the opposite chair.

"I must say, you took a rather circuitous and dangerous route to reach me, *monsieur*."

It was Carter's turn to smile. "How is Pepe?"

"In agony, but mending. I'm afraid his young friend will have to hand-feed him for several weeks."

"A pity. Of course you know it isn't you I want to reach."

"That is what I've been told." He drank, his narrow eyes evaluating Carter over the rim of the glass. "Of course, I cannot say for sure that I can reach the lady in question."

"Of course not."

"Indeed, if, after our talk this evening, I were ever accused of even knowing the lady, I would emphatically deny it."

Carter nodded. "Just as you would deny being anything but a successful attorney, or deny that you have probably financed all her schemes as well as those of half the criminals in Europe."

"Hearsay, Monsieur Carter, hearsay. Proof? There has never been a shred."

"And I'm sure there never will be. I have to see Serena."

"May I ask, assuming of course that I could reach her, what is your business?"

It was time to stop playing games. Carter took out his wallet. From it he extracted his agency ID and his high-level authorization to use any and all military assistance anywhere in the world.

DuPree's eyes narrowed as he examined them very, very closely and then handed them back. "You are—how do they say in America—a very heavy hitter, Monsieur Carter."

"I am."

"Then I assume it is government business you wish to discuss with Serena?"

"It is: security, the highest clearance."

"You know, of course, she no longer dabbles in that sort of thing."

"I've heard, but she may be able to help me find what I'm looking for."

"She may." He nodded. "For a price. You know Serena does nothing without some recompense."

"I'm familiar with how the lady works."

"Very well," he said, getting to his feet. "How shall I make you known to her?"

"Just my name will be enough."

"I doubt that, but I shall try. If you will excuse me?"

He was gone the length of two more drinks, and when he returned, he had a puzzled smile on his face.

"She will meet you. In fact, she looks forward to it. Most unusual, considering her present difficulties. You must have made a lasting impression on her."

"I did," Carter drawled lazily. "I didn't kill her when I should have."

"Charming," DuPree said and spread a map on the table between them. "How well do you know the coast of Cornwall, England . . . ?"

"Weatherby . . . Carter here."

"You found her, I can tell by your voice."

"Not quite, but I've got a meet. I've still got to convince her to help us, and that might be difficult . . . honor among thieves and all that crap. Where's Androssov?"

"Still in Paris, but we think he's getting ready to make a move."

"Good, don't lose him. I'm flying to Cherbourg tonight. Have someone drive Tamara over, and set us both up with like name passports."

"Where are you headed?"

"England, for now. We'll take the SeaLink from Cherbourg to Weymouth. I'll meet her at the Hôtel Mercure Cherbourg. It's near the Gare Maritime."

"Don't you think that may be risky? She's a hot number for them right now. They'll be watching every commercial way out of France. You may be spotted."

"I know," Carter replied, "that's the idea."

ELEVEN

Carter consulted the map on the dash before him and pushed the boat's throttles up another couple of knots.

It was a clear day, only moderately cloudy and a calm sea running. The coast of Cornwall was beautifully ominous, with its high cliffs melding into rocky, jagged beaches.

The room at the Mercure Cherbourg had been bandbox modern but comfortable. The lounge was cozy, and the food, served on an outside terrace overlooking the quay, had been excellent.

"We are highly exposed," Tamara had said, sliding into her chair and darting a quick look around at the other diners.

"That's the idea. Recognize anyone?"

"No, but I have an idea I will pretty soon. I'm bait, right?"

"Right, and a diversion when the time comes."

Later, in the room, she had made overtures . . . real ones.

"The SeaLink leaves at six in the morning," he had said gently. "I think we'd better get some sleep."

Throughout the four-hour boat trip, she still didn't spot anyone. But Carter's senses were on "high." They were being watched; he could feel it.

In the English seaport of Weymouth, he rented a sleek BMW and they headed toward Exeter on the A30, where they stopped for lunch.

"What do you think?" Tamara asked.

"I think they've picked us up, but they're tracking us by phone," Carter growled.

"Then you could lose them?"

"I could, but there's no percentage. I want to find out if they are after me . . . or you."

"How sweet of you," she said, her face losing a few shades of color.

Just short of Land's End, he cut off the A30 north to St. Ives. It was in season, so only a healthy bribe got them a hotel room.

"What now?"

"We take a boat excursion of St. Ives Bay."

The tour was two hours long. Halfway through it, at Carbis, in the deepest part of the bay, the crowd left the boat for tea in an old inn.

Carter pulled a map from his pocket. "I'll be leaving you here," he said to an astonished Tamara. "Get back on board with the crowd. When you dock at St. Ives, walk the streets, stay in crowds. Start calling our room at the hotel at nine o'clock. If I'm not back by midnight, don't go to the hotel. Take the car and drive to Truro . . . here. There's an American pub at Twenty-one Prince Albert Street. Ask for Carl, he'll know what to do."

She accepted the map and the keys to the BMW without a word. When the crowd left the inn to return to the boat, she was with them.

Carter wasn't.

He was making his way to the Hoyle Inlet and a boat that Carl Frobisher had already arranged for his use.

Within twenty minutes after leaving the inn, he was speeding north and east up the coast of Cornwall.

It was almost dusk now, but Carter shunned the use of running lights as he turned into the wide mouth of Trevone Bay. Once inside, he navigated by the coastline rearing into the sky.

There were several coves dipping inland from the bay, guarded by narrow channels passable only during high tide.

He counted them off with flashes from the deck spotlight. When he found the one he wanted, he switched off the spot and shot through.

Inside was another bay, more like a lagoon actually, with tall, slick-sided cliffs on three sides. Directly in front of him he spotted the gleaming white hull of a big sixty-foot yacht and throttled the little cruiser down.

With the inboard in neutral, he let his momentum swing him around the fantail. One more fast sweep of the light identified the *Gypsy*.

Satisfied, he engaged the prop and idled to the yacht's starboard side. About twenty feet short of the halfmast gangway, he reversed.

"Ahoy, *Gypsy*!"

"What is your business?"

"I have an appointment with the lady!"

Three crew members in gleaming whites moved to the rail above him. *"Votre nom, monsieur.* You have a name?"

"Carter."

The gangway started down at once.

The Killmaster slid in close, tied the boat off, and climbed the gangway.

"Right down that ladder and to your right, *monsieur.*"

He followed directions and knocked lightly on a paneled door. It was opened by a young boy who was built like an Olympic weightlifter and bare to the waist. Each move he made was accompanied by rippling muscles along his arms and across his chest. His dark skin had such a sheen to it that Carter knew it was oiled. His twin stood at the far end of the cabin, beside a gaudy, maroon-colored round bed piled high with pillows of every size and shape.

Lounging in regal splendor atop the bed was the gypsy woman herself, Serena.

"I thought you weren't coming, Nick, darling. But thank God you have, you're just in time. Get out!" she snapped at the two boys.

The two sets of muscles threw withering glances at Carter

and exited quickly, closing the door behind them.

"Well, don't just stand there, Nick," she said, throwing her arms wide in the air. The movement made her enormous breasts do a crazy dance beneath something filmy and wafting. "Do we kiss for old times' sake, or do we start clawing at each other?"

Carter slid his arms around her and surrendered to a feverish kiss. He finally managed to extricate himself before she smothered him, and stepped back to study her, with his hands on her shoulders.

"Passion, huh?" she chuckled.

He nodded. "Yeah, you're still a good actress."

"Want me or a drink?"

"Appreciate it, Serena, but let's start with a drink. Scotch—"

"Three fingers, one cube." She undulated across the room toward a built-in bar. "Still in the spook business?"

"Too young to retire, too old to get out of it," he replied, shaking a cigarette from his pack and lighting it. "How's the crime business?"

"Slow," she said with a laugh. She mixed her conception of two drinks, which was hardly normal, and returned to Carter.

After handing him his glass, she arranged herself on a chaise in a seated position, with her feet pulled up under her thighs and her knees spread wide.

No matter where he looked there was tantalizing flesh, and even though his body should have been totally satiated, he found that he could not make his eyes avoid her. He gave up trying and raised his glass.

"Cheers."

"To sin," she replied and drained half her drink. "Well, tell me what's on your mind and then we'll get down to what's on mine."

Carter had to laugh. Serena hadn't changed a bit. But he knew that under all that beauty and sexual bantering, there was a woman without a shred of morality, pity for her fellow human, or the shred of a heart.

Serafina Gamboli, alias Serena, the gypsy woman, was a stately female with a ripe, Junoesque figure. She had full, naturally red lips and dark, burning eyes, in a lovely face in which, however, her surprisingly small nose seemed to be out of proportion. Its sauciness did not somehow fit her otherwise impressive appearance. Her hair was silky blue-black, and was expertly and artistically arranged every day in the form of a regal crown, accentuating the paleness of her long face. When she chose to loosen the coiffure, the hair fell down to her knees, creating the impression of an angel with a black halo and deep dark wings.

Carter knew from experience that she was no angel, but he had to admit, she was still one impressive woman.

She had to be at least fourty-four or forty-five years old, but her face and body looked fifteen years younger.

"I need a favor."

"So do I." The smile was dazzling, but coupled with the amount of flesh she was exposing, it became almost obscene.

"Business before pleasure, okay?" Carter countered.

"Ah, we get down to it." The smile faded; the eyes narrowed. She leaned forward, making her breasts sway nearly to her knees. "If it's business, what's in it for me?"

Carter relaxed. She had said what he wanted to hear. If there was one thing Serena was more interested in than sex, it was the accumulation of money.

"A very great deal." He paused, forcing her to meet his gaze. "Who took the Ritz in Paris?"

One eyebrow arched sharply. "That's a tricky question. Why do you think I would know?"

"Because, if you weren't behind it yourself, I think you can find out who was."

She spoke very slowly, choosing her words carefully. "I've heard it was a very pro job."

"It was."

"The police have no leads."

"That's right."

"And there hasn't been a whisper—at least, one I've heard—of any of the pros I know being involved."

"That doesn't mean you couldn't get a whisper if you put out feelers. It's a fat finder's fee, Serena . . . very fat."

Carter could almost see the wheels turning in her perfectly coiffed head. She got up, freshened the drinks, and this time when she returned to the bed she dispensed with the erotic pose.

"How fat a finder's fee, Nick?"

"Between the reward my people would be willing to pay, and what the Ritz insurance will offer to get their customers' precious personal possessions back, I'd say it would be close to a million."

Her heavy eyebrows shot up, and she took a quick sip of her drink to cover any other facial reaction that would give away her surprise.

"Dollars?"

"Dollars."

"That's a very interesting proposition. What did they get that you are so interested in?"

"I can't tell you that."

"Is it solid?"

"Yes."

"They might have already fenced it."

"Maybe," he said. "But if I find out who the originals are, I can trace the fence."

"True." Serena finished her drink and carefully set the glass aside. "If you're involved, and your people are willing to pay that kind of money, the article must be very valuable."

"It is. National security, top drawer."

"Then," she said and grinned, "it might be worth a mil and a half?"

"No dickering, Serena. I'm not even sure of the million. It's just an educated guess, but I think I can swing it."

She nodded and got to her feet. "Make yourself comfortable. I've got to make a couple of ship-to-shore calls."

As she left, there was no sexual undulation to the walk. It was a calm, purposeful stride: the businesswoman going about her business.

Carter shed his jacket and topped off his drink. It was almost an hour later before Serena returned to find him pacing.

"Nervous, Nick? That's not like you."

"That's right," he growled, "so you know this is big. Well?"

"I've put some of my people, here and in France, on it. I'd say it's better than a fifty-fifty chance they'll come up with something. Now I need a favor, besides the money."

"Name it."

"There's a fat cat from Morocco throwing a party at his villa in Deauville next week, to open the season."

"So?"

"So I'm invited. You are, too. He's legit, but he likes to associate with shady people like me. My contacts will also be at the party."

"But you can't get into France."

"That's the favor," she said, moving toward the huge bed. "Clear it for me, and don't tell me you can't. I know you can. I need help to go to that party for personal business reasons. You help me, I help you."

"Then we have a deal?"

Her fingers tugged here and there, and the wispy gown fell to the floor. Her nude body slid onto the bed like a lithe cat, and the smile on her full lips was as Cheshire as they come.

"Almost, Nick . . . almost."

She stretched, her breasts rising as one arm reached and slid along the headboard toward a switch. The lights were dimmed, with just enough illumination to make each other out, enough to find each other and operate by.

Carter knew exactly what she meant, and he had to admit

he had been thinking about the same thing since the moment he had stepped into the cabin.

He finished his drink and stood by the bed, fumbling at his clothing, watching Serena's nude body writhe. The exhilaration of her agreement to his proposition evolved into physical lust by the time he, too, was naked.

He knelt over her. His mouth was suddenly dry, ashes dry. She pulled him down and rolled toward him on her hip. They collided between their hips, and the touch brought a groan to both their lips.

"Nick!" His name was like a command as she grabbed one of his wrists and brought his hand to a breast.

He let her press the hand and then cover it with her own to guide the kneading fingers. Her eyes closed tightly and she shuddered.

He could feel her heart beat wildly in her chest. Her breasts were hard, with swollen nipples. Her face was distorted with clawing need.

"Now," she whispered, "now!"

But before he could comply, she rolled over him and took him herself. Her body heaved until she had adjusted herself so that their lips met and her breasts were crushed against his chest.

"Nick . . . oh, Nick," she whispered.

And then her wildly gyrating body managed to drive all thoughts from his mind, leaving only desire.

He put his hands on her sides, high up under her arms, and stroked slowly downward, sweeping into the narrowness of her waist, flaring them out to accommodate the flare of her thrusting hips. He stroked all the way down the sides of her legs as far as he could reach.

She shivered and groaned, writhing atop him as his hands started back up, this time along her inner thighs.

Then he found her buttocks and let loose the animal in him.

"Oh, my God!" she cried.

Then it was downhill for both of them. Carter held her to

him until the shuddering paroxysms that wracked her form subsided.

At last she curled herself against him, utterly spent, relaxed as a kitten.

"God, what a waste!"

"What waste?" Carter said, letting reality wash back over his mind.

"Not seeing you for years."

"Just don't forget our little bargain."

"Just start figuring my finder's fee! I'll call you tomorrow. Where will you be?"

"London, the Piccadilly, under the name of Carstairs."

"One question?"

"Yeah?"

"Is the other side looking for the article as well?"

Carter had purposely not told her of the KGB's involvement. She was smart enough not to get in the middle if both the biggies were involved.

"No," he lied.

"You're lying."

Carter rolled his face to the side. "Tell you what . . ."

"What?"

"If you get in the middle and get hurt, I'll add another two hundred thou to the fee."

"What if I get killed?"

"Then you'll be remembered for your heroic act of patriotism."

"Know what, Nick?"

"What?"

"You," she whispered, kissing the tip of his nose, "are the biggest son of a bitch I have ever known."

Carter started to reply, but her hips were already starting to move again.

He didn't bother speaking.

He was already being swallowed up in the pure animal of her.

TWELVE

London was unseasonably hot and muggy, with a near foglike haze that seemed to envelop everything and everyone in its gray grip.

Together they checked into the Piccadilly. It was the perfect hotel, not first class, but comfortable. It was highly transient, in the heart of everything, and Carter knew its layout, down to every entrance and exit, like the back of his hand.

"Will that be cash or charge, Mr. Carstairs?"

"Cash. I hate credit cards," Carter replied.

"Then there will be a slight deposit needed, sir."

The Killmaster laid a hundred-pound note on the counter. "Will that be slight enough?"

"More than sufficient, sir. Room Twelve-oh-one."

Carter accepted the key and rejoined Tamara at the tobacco-magazine kiosk. "The elevator is this way," he said, gathering their two bags and moving away.

She followed him without a word.

The elevator was small, just large enough for them and their bags. As it started to rise, she finally spoke.

"We've got one."

"Where?" he said, not trying to hide the surprise in his voice. He had checked the entire lobby, and he was pretty sure he hadn't spotted a soul that would fit the profile.

123

"The tall, buxom, horse-faced woman at the theater ticket booth."

"The one with the umbrella and funny hat?"

Tamara nodded. "She's an English maid at the Soviet embassy."

"But not English?"

"Polish, but without a trace of an accent. Her name is Freya Kanovski. She took her training in Moscow. That's how I know her file."

Carter nodded as the elevator door opened. "We'll bring her on as soon as I've made some calls."

In the room, he dropped the bags and made for the phone. "Get out of that dress and into some slacks," he murmured to Tamara, "in case you have to move fast."

She dug into her bag while he relayed the Paris AXE number that would bring only Weatherby's voice onto the line.

"Here."

"Mr. W, this is Mr. C."

"Where are you?"

"At the Pic in London. I've contacted the lady, and she agrees. Can you pull a string or two? She would like to sample some Camembert and a few local Norman wines by next week."

"I think it can be done."

"Good, what's the situation on our late guest?"

"He's developed a sudden interest in history."

"For instance?"

"The tapestry in Bayeaux."

"I see. Has he made contact?"

"Yes, we're keeping track of two others."

"Our lady friends?" Carter asked.

"No, but I am hopeful."

"I'll check back this evening."

He killed the connection and turned to Tamara. She had shed the light summer dress she had been wearing and replaced it with a pair of dark blue slacks and a crisp white linen blouse.

"Androssov is in Bayeaux."

Her look was vacant for a moment while her mind flipped geographical index cards. "That's Normandy. Do you think they have located the thieves?"

"We'll soon find out," Carter growled. He explained what he wanted her to do, and what he would be doing in the next hour.

By the time he had finished, her jaw was set, her body rigid, and there was a gaze in the two black marbles of her eyes very akin to hate.

"So if Madame Freya Kanovski tries to take me for interrogation, you can assume they think we know more than they do. If she merely tries to terminate me, then you can assume they already have a lead and have no use for me."

"That's about it," Carter replied, lighting a cigarette to project the cool he didn't feel.

Tamara Petrovna shrugged. "All right, I'll be bait."

"You did want to come along."

"Yes, I did. Only I thought that you felt . . ." Her eyes fell, and she suddenly became very involved with the bracelet on her wrist.

"Felt what, Tamara?"

"Nothing. I can handle her."

Carter took the elevator to the lobby and paused to peruse a *Times* with one eye while he checked the populace out with the other.

There were two of them, one short, with a glass eye and a baggy summer suit, the other medium height, with a trimmed beard and a camera around his neck bouncing against a Day-Glow shirt. He was getting a shoeshine just outside the hotel's main entrance. Baggy Pants was looking at posters at the theater ticket kiosk, where Madame Kanovski had been spotted.

They were obviously the woman's backup, but not in her league. The eye contact between them was not covert enough, and Baggy Pants was making Carter far too much with his good eye not to be obvious.

The tall, horse-faced woman was not in sight.

Carter paid for the *Times,* moved out to the sidewalk, and paused to light a cigarette. Out of the corner of his eye, he saw Baggy Pants strolling casually across the lobby. Day-Glow was absorbed in his shoes. Just beyond him, at the curb, was a taxi stand.

"Grotons," Carter said as he crawled into the back of the cab. "It's a pub on upper Charing Cross Road. Do you know it?"

"I can find it, mate" came the chuckling reply.

Just as the cab pulled away, Carter turned slightly in time to see Day-Glow nod toward the interior of the lobby. Through the tall windows, Carter saw the one-eyed man sprint to a bank of pay phones along the wall.

The cab made a turn.

"Stop here!"

"Here, mate?"

"Here," Carter growled and dropped a ten-pound note onto the front seat. "Take yourself a short drive to another stand somewhere, but don't go back to the Piccadilly for at least an hour. All right?"

"Right, mate . . . what the hell."

The Killmaster speed-walked around the full block and came up behind the hotel at the delivery entrance.

A long-haired young man lounged in the pedestrian doorway, smoking a cigarette.

"Help ya, sir?" he asked as Carter moved by him sideways.

"Wife's in the lobby. Got a bird on another floor," Carter whispered, winking conspiratorially. "You know what I mean?"

"Sure, mate." The young man grinned knowingly. "Do one fer me!"

Carter took the service elevator to the tenth floor and stairs on up to the twelfth. The hall was clear, and there was no sound on the other side of the door to 1201.

Four doors down, on the opposite side of the hall, was a maids' utility closet. Carter jimmied it, stepped inside, and closed the door, leaving a millimeter crack for his eye.

Less than five minutes later, a tall woman in a blue maid's uniform passed by, carrying towels over one arm.

When she stopped at 1201 and made a three-quarter turn, Carter could see her face.

It was Freya Kanovski.

"Maid, mum . . . extra towels," she said, rapping lightly on the door to 1201 and then entering.

Carter had to steel himself not to rush the door. That would have been useless.

He cursed himself, and the way things had to be, as he took the service elevator to the basement.

The lank-haired young man was still lounging in the doorway.

"Stood ya up, did she?" he leered.

"Guess it's just not my day," Carter said and shrugged.

He stepped out into the haze and headed away from the hotel at a brisk pace.

He hoped it was Tamara Petrovna's day. He hoped she could handle the woman without his help. He *couldn't* help. If he did, Tamara wouldn't be put on the spot, forced to make her own decision. And Carter couldn't be sure just where she stood.

Damn, he thought, *what this business will turn you into . . . a cold, bloodless bastard.*

He walked for over an hour and then found a phone booth.

"Room Twelve-oh-one, please." She answered on the first ring. "How are things?"

"I'm alive, you bastard."

"I was just calling myself that."

"You'd better get back up here. We have some cleaning up to do."

He broke the connection and called the London AXE hot line, identifying himself quickly.

"What do you need, N3?"

"A housecleaning crew at the Piccadilly Hotel, Room Twelve-oh-one. One package."

"We'll take care of it."

"Bring three empties. One for the currest package. A lady and myself will be going out the same way in the morning."

"Will do."

Five minutes later, Carter was back in the room.

One look told him everything. Freya Kanovski lay facedown, the hilt of a stiletto jutting from her throat just under the chin.

There were only a few drops of blood on the front of her uniform.

Tamara stood by the window, a drink in her hand. On the table beside her was a short-barreled .25-caliber, silenced Beretta. Not much of a weapon for distance, but up close one slug in the back of the neck and it was all over.

"Satisfied?" she said in a low, even voice.

"Satisfied," Carter replied. "No more games. You're on my side. Did she try for you?"

Tamara nodded. "Got off one shot. The hole is in the ceiling, there."

Carter found it. "I've got a crew coming. They'll take care of it." He poured himself a drink and folded into a chair. "Sorry."

She shrugged. "At least now you know."

"Yeah. Now I know that they really want you dead, and I can guess that they've got a lot more on the Madonna than we do—"

He was interrupted by a rap on the door.

Tamara retreated to the bathroom while Carter answered the knock.

"Yes?"

"Hamilton Cartage Service, sir."

Carter opened the door and stepped aside. There were

three of them, all in coveralls with the logo of a speeding truck on their breast pockets and HAMILTON CARTAGE across their backs.

"Room clean?"

Carter nodded. "You can talk."

"Very clean hit," said the one kneeling on the floor by the woman. "You haven't lost your touch, N3."

Carter didn't explain what actually happened.

"What time will you want to go out in the morning?"

"Around ten," Carter replied. "There's a BMW across the street, rented. It will have to be turned in."

"We'll pick you up by ten. Destination?"

"Anywhere around Deauville. There's an airfield near there, small. Can you get a charter out of Heathrow or Gatwick?"

"Better yet, a rental. One of our own boys can fly it."

They placed the two empty crates against one wall and moved Freya Kanovski out in the third. Carter closed the door behind them and heard Tamara emerge from the bathroom.

"Your people are very efficient."

"About the same as yours."

"About," she cooly replied, lifting the telephone receiver from its cradle. "What would you like for lunch?"

Carter knew that whatever intimacy had been between them was now over.

Serena's call rang through just after eight o'clock.

Her voice on the phone had a strange, quivering quality in it. It was unlike Serena to stammer or falter in her thought or speech.

Carter recognized the quality of the sound and didn't like it. It represented fear.

"Something's wrong, Serena. What is it?"

"The other side," she replied. "They've got word out all over England and France . . . your description, and the description of a woman who's supposed to be with you."

"What about it?"

"There's fifty thousand on both of you, and they don't care how the hit is made."

"That goes with the game, Serena, you know that."

She sighed. "Yeah, Nick, I guess I do. I think I'm just getting too old for this crap, that's all."

"What have you got for me?" he replied in the coldest voice he could muster.

"A little, not much. I can get more, lots more, at the party. I've talked to Cadiz—that's the Moroccan's name. We're both welcome, and he can't wait to see me."

"Good. Now what little do you have, Serena?"

"Can I sail into *la belle* France?"

"You can. It's set."

"Okay. Ever hear of Myron Porthal?"

"Never."

"You wouldn't. He keeps a very low profile. He's a gem dealer, has offices in Amsterdam, South Africa, and operates personally out of a very ritzy address on the Avenue Victor Hugo in Deauville."

"Carriage trade?"

"Right, but even the carriage trade likes bargains. He's put the word out to several people that he might have a very large shipment soon of bargain-basement stones."

Carter felt a tingle along his spine that raised the hairs on the back of his neck. "You think the shipment may have come by way of the Ritz's safe-deposit boxes?"

"It may. There's a ninety-nine-percent chance that Porthal will be at the Cadiz party tomorrow night. It's right up his alley. We're old friends. I might find out his source. And there's something else. What kind of equipment was used on the boxes? You said you had read the police report."

"I did," Carter replied.

"Describe."

He did, in detail, to the best of his memory.

"I thought so. It sounds too clean to be electric, and too

slow to be a common small-base drill. Ever hear of a Selston laser drill?''

"Vaguely. Developed in West Germany, wasn't it? Used almost exclusively in the aircraft industry for fast, delicate work on airplane skin, even the space shuttle.''

"Right on the head, my spook friend. I only know of two men in our line of work who really know how to handle one: Luigi Pondetti, and an old drunk named Dino Foche. I put out questionnaires on both of them.''

"And?''

"Pondetti got religion. He works security for the Vatican now, and the word is he hasn't been out of Vatican City in two years.''

"Can you be sure of that?''

"Fairly sure. If he steps outside the pope's prerogative, he's looking at twenty years as the guest of the Italian government.''

"And Dino Foche?''

"Still a drunk, but suddenly prosperous. He bought himself a boat. Lives in the habor at Honfleur, and likes to entertain young ladies with expensive tastes.''

"And he wasn't always like that?''

"Not in the five years I've known him. Matter of fact, I turned him down for a petty job six months ago, even when he offered to do it for a flat rate.''

"I'll check him out tomorrow.''

"Tread with caution, Nick. He's a touchy little rabbit, and he'll run like one if he sees your type.''

"I'll use someone else.''

"The woman you're supposed to be traveling with?''

"Maybe.''

"Is she built like me, Nick?'' Serena asked, chuckling.

"Is anybody?'' he replied dryly. "Where do I meet you?''

"I'm anchoring at Villerville, and taking the launch over to Trouville-Deauville. The quay at ten o'clock?''

"Until then.''

He hung up and turned toward the bed. Tamara was on her side, turned away from him.

Extra sheets, a pillow, and a blanket were piled on the sofa.

THIRTEEN

Pierre Donet closed the door marked PORTHAL: FINE GEMS and walked toward the casino with a broad smile on his handsome face. He was pleased with himself.

The deal was set. The exchange would be made the next afternoon. Porthal had agreed to take everything but two strings of pearls, a large brooch that turned out to be filled with fake stones, and the odd icon of the Mother and Child.

Porthal was a cautious man, but that was all for the best. Donet knew Carmont would approve of the method: a twilight round of golf at the Hôtel du Golf club. The tee of the fifth hole intersected with the green of the fourteenth.

Carmont would tee off of the fifth as Porthal and his partner putted the fourteenth. When both had finished, each would walk on with the other's bag and clubs.

Donet checked his watch. His shift didn't start at the casino for over an hour. More than enough time to stop at Robère's for a quick drink and call Julian.

He found a table near the back of the bar and adjacent to the two pay phones. When he had ordered, he slipped into one of the booths and dialed.

"Yes."

"Marta, Pierre. Is Julian there?"

"Yes, one moment."

Donet didn't miss the tightness in the woman's voice. She and Julian had obviously been arguing again. Donet only hoped they didn't split—or, worse yet, kill each other—before all the money was accumulated and divided up.

Pierre Donet was sick and tired of being a croupier, and more than ready for an early retirement.

"Pierre, how did it go?"

"Excellent. The bastard drives a hard bargain, but he has agreed to our terms." Donet went on to explain what Porthal wouldn't buy and the method of exchanging the money for the stones the following day.

"Cautious little man, isn't he?"

"He is," Donet replied, "but he is also trustworthy."

"We'll get the goods off the boat just before dawn in the morning. I'll inform Dino and Carmine to sail with the early morning tide."

"*Au revoir, mon ami.*—Tomorrow we are rich!"

His drink was waiting at the table when he sat down.

"Does *monsieur* have a light?"

Donet looked up and smiled. "*Mais oui, mademoiselle.*" He produced his lighter and moved the flame to the tip of her cigarette.

Even sitting on the barstool, he could see that she was tall and sleek, like a palomino colt. The hair was a lustrous blond, and the deep tan of her shoulders in the summer dress was a contrasting bronze.

"*Merci, monsieur,*" she said and smiled. "You are here for the season?"

"No, I am afraid I work here, at the casino."

"Oh? You are a gambler?"

"I work for the casino, as a croupier. I never gamble. Please, join me."

"*Merci.*"

She slid from the stool and into the chair across from him like a graceful cat, placing her purse very near his arm.

In his mind, Donet compared this rangy beauty to the buxom Claudia Biget that he lived with. In comparison, Claudia was a cow.

"I would stay the season, but I cannot afford to," the beautiful blonde pouted. "You are so lucky to live all the time in a resort like Deauville."

"Not so lucky," Donet said with a shrug. "Deauville is quite boring most of the time."

"Pardon, monsieur?" she said, leaning forward and cocking her head. In the process, she pushed the purse closer to his side of the table.

"I said, Deauville can be quite boring at times."

"Perhaps, if one is lonely."

There it was, the invitation, in her voice and in those cool green eyes.

"Then *mademoiselle* is lonely?"

"Very."

"I finish my shift at midnight. Perhaps we could meet somewhere," Donet said, already manufacturing an excuse to send Claudia home from the casino alone.

"I think I would like that," she breathed huskily, turning the full wattage of those eyes in his direction.

"Shall we say, here, at twelve-thirty?" Donet said, feeling his pulse quicken.

"I shall be here, *monsieur,* but now I must go. *Au revoir.*"

"Au revoir."

The departure was so abrupt it left Pierre Donet's mouth hanging open.

Then he suddenly realized he didn't even know her name.

Sophia Dobroskov walked slowly from the café, but the moment her heels found the sidewalk her long legs began to move.

At last success! After days of watching every buyer of stolen goods they could unearth, they now knew the fence used by the Ritz thieves.

She retraced the way back to Avenue Victor Hugo, passed Porthal's shop, and darted into the open door of a cream BMW.

"What about him?" Eva Stalnik asked from the driver's side of the car.

"He's one of them. I'm sure I recognized the voice."

"God, I hope so. We've followed eight men from that shop just today. Let's hear it!"

Sophia lifted a small recorder from her purse, reversed the tape, and then hit the "play" button.

Only half the conversation had gone by before Eva was smiling broadly.

"It is the tall one who worked in the safe-deposit-box room with the woman loading the bags."

Sophia nodded. "I agree. Myron Porthal is our man."

"Stay here, watch the shop," Eva said, starting the car. "I'll get Maurice!"

Julian Carmont replaced the phone, picked up his drink, and turned to face Marta. "It's set for tomorrow afternoon."

"How is the exchange to be made?"

Carmont moved behind her at the bar and freshened his drink. At the same time, he explained how the switch was to be made and what they would have to do leading up to it.

"I will notify Carmine tonight that you will join him and Dino on the boat. You will sail at high tide in the morning. That should be about four. When you reach the Deauville-Trouville quay, you and Carmine can taxi up to the hotel with the suitcase. Keep it in your room. I will arrive around two in the afternoon to make the switch of the gems to my golf bag."

He paused, his forehead furrowed in concentration as he thought about the next steps before verbalizing them.

Excellent, Marta mused. *Julian Carmont has everything planned out down to the last detail. He never puts himself in jeopardy at any time. If there is a hitch in the plans, he never*

*has his hands on the loot more than a half hour at the most,
and that on a golf course where he could dispose of it at once
in a lake, or pond, or in the woods.* She and Carmine would
be exposing themselves for a much longer time if the police
had somehow gotten on their trail.

"Marta . . ."

"Yes? Sorry, my mind was wandering. We make the
switch to your golf bag in my room at two o'clock."

"Exactly. I will get a three-o'clock tee time, so that should
put me on the fifth tee perfectly in place to meet Porthal."

"I know nothing of golf bags," Marta said, her eyes
searching his for a hint of the double cross she knew he was
planning. She detected nothing. "Will everything fit into one
bag?"

"It should be no problem . . . lots of pockets, and if
necessary, I will discard a few of the clubs. Now, Porthal has
refused the diamond and ruby brooch, the pearls, and the
little religious statue of the Mother and Child. I will instruct
Carmine to dispose of them at sea." He paused, and his eyes
narrowed as he stared at her intently. "And the both of you
know what else to dispose of, don't you, Marta?"

She felt her spine tighten. It had been part of the plan from
the very beginning that Dino Foche would never see a dime of
the loot. He was the one weak link they had, the one who
couldn't be trusted to keep his mouth shut no matter what
happened.

She and Carmine would kill Dino Foche and dispose of his
body at sea on the way to the Deauville quay. *Once again,
they do the dirty work while Julian Carmont keeps his hands
clean.*

"We'll take care of it, Julian, but about the other . . ."

"What other?"

"The pearls are negligible, and the stones in the brooch are
fake, we know. But the icon?"

"Religious artifcats belong to churches, Marta. They are
highly registered and can be easily traced. Porthal is no fool,
and neither am I."

"But the icon could be very valuable. Perhaps a collector?"

"No," Carmont said firmly. "It goes overboard with Dino. Understand?"

Marta shrugged her shoulders but hid her eyes from his by turning to the room, away from the bar where he stood glaring at her.

"If you say so," she murmured.

"I do."

"I'd best get going if I'm to get to the hotel, change, and drive to Honfleur."

She slid from the stool and gathered her purse and the green lamé jacket that matched her ankle-length gown.

"If you had worn something simple—slacks, or a dress—instead of that, you wouldn't have to return to the hotel."

"I thought, Julian, that perhaps we would dine together tonight."

"You know that's impossible just now, my dear," he said, forcing a smile and taking the bite out of his voice. "We can't be seen together in public until this is all over."

"Of course," Marta replied dryly.

Julian moved with her to the door, his hand at the back of her neck, the fingers kneading. It was all Marta could do not to fling it away.

"You're tense, my dear. Relax. Tomorrow it will be all over. We will be rich."

"Yes, rich," she murmured. "Then what, Julian?"

"What?" He smiled. "Anything! We resume our lives, but on a much higher plane. With enough money, anything is possible!"

"Of course."

She gave him a perfunctory kiss by brushing his lips with her own, and left. When she was safely away, she sighed deeply.

Julian was a good actor. She had detected not one trace of nervousness or apprehension in his manner. There was no hint in his voice or in his demeanor that he planned on leaving all of them holding the bag.

Marta hoped that she had done an equal job of acting, not letting Julian suspect that she knew.

Some of it, of course, was supposition, but she felt that she had seen enough evidence of his perfidity in the past. She had known Julian for a long time, known him very intimately . . . intimately enough to know—or guess—where in the apartment he would hide something he wanted no one to see.

She had arrived an hour early that evening. Julian was still in his shower.

"You're early, darling!" he called. "Fix yourself a drink. I'll be out in a few minutes."

It took her less than two minutes to find his little cache: the canceled lease on the boutique, along with the receipt of sale on all the merchandise, as well as a money order in English pounds for the sale of both his automobiles.

If that weren't enough to tell her that Julian planned to flee, she also found a one-way air ticket to Rio via Lisbon out of Paris and the contract for a rental car that he had picked up that afternoon.

The contract called for the car to be dropped off in Paris the next evening. The flight to Lisbon was also the next evening.

The cash from the robbery that they had already split was sizable. But Porthal's payment for the gems would be fifty times that amount.

Tomorrow, on the Hôtel du Golf course, Julian Carmont would be picking up enough cash to keep himself in high style for the rest of his life.

If he could keep it all.

And Marta Penn was positive that Julian planned on doing just that.

But she didn't care. She had her own ace in the hole: the ivory statue of the Madonna and Child.

She had seen icons just like it in the private collection of one of her old lovers from London. They had each been worth a king's ransom. Marta had a sneaking suspicion that the icon resting right then in the bilges of a boat in Honfleur harbor was also worth a fortune.

She had no intention of throwing it into the sea. If Julian planned on leaving the others holding the bag, she had no intention of holding it with them.

Marta left the building containing Carmont's apartment by a rear door and walked the three blocks to her car. A half block short of it, she paused at a phone booth.

She dialed the number from memory, and a valet answered the phone.

"I'm sorry, but Monsieur Cadiz cannot come to the phone at this moment."

"You tell him Marta Penn wants to talk to him. He'll come to the phone."

She was right. Seconds later, the cultured, modulated voice of the first man she had conquered as a young girl came over the line.

"Marta, my darling, where are you calling from?"

"Here in Deauville," she replied gaily. "You suave lecher, you're having a party tonight. Why wasn't I invited?"

"I thought you would be in London or on the Riviera. It has been years, Marta, my sweet . . . I've missed you."

"Then I'm invited?"

"You shall be my guest of honor."

"Wonderful. *Ciao*, Sedji."

Marta walked the rest of the way to her car with a light, bouncy step.

She had a far better reason for wearing the elaborate ball gown she now wore than for a private dinner with Julian Carmont.

Myron Porthal turned on both burglar alarms, locked the front door, and set off at a brisk pace for his apartment on the Avenue de la République.

He had just an hour to shave and change clothes for Cadiz's party. And what a party it would be. If all went well this evening, he would have connections for over half the stones he would pick up on the golf course the following day.

By the time Porthal reached his block, he was humming to himself. He was almost at his building, his key in his hand, when a woman's voice stopped him.

"Pardon, monsieur."

The voice came from below. The basement entrance was under the front stairs, and a short, steep flight of steps led down to it from the sidewalk.

Porthal had a moment of apprehension. In his business, he had made many enemies. But he could not remember if any of them were women.

"Yes?"

A tall, dark-haired woman moved up the steps and stopped very close to Porthal. She wore a silky, clinging dress over the most striking figure Myron Porthal had ever seen.

"What do you want, *mademoiselle*?"

"I have been told, by mutual friends, that you sometimes buy gems without asking the seller for a written release."

"What friends?" Porthal asked cooly. "I don't know what you're talking about. I am a reputable dealer. If you want to discuss business—legitimate business, of course—you will find me in my shop at ten o'clock Monday morning."

Her question had been a surprise. From her looks and her approach, he had assumed her to be a whore.

It was too bad she wasn't, he thought, as her perfume invaded his senses. It was a musky scent that only brunettes could wear, and it was having its effect on his aging body. Her hand, warm and firm on his, was also having an effect.

"My friends are in the car right behind you, Monsieur Porthal. Why don't you join us in the car for a few seconds?"

"I'll do no such—"

Suddenly she was pressed against him, her left hand curled in the front of his shirt. Her other hand was holding something sharp that slid through the thin material of his shirt. It jabbed him painfully in the ribs near the center of his chest.

"Not a sound," she said in a low and suddenly menacing voice. "Do as I tell you or I will push the point of this knife into your heart. You won't feel it and it won't hurt, but you will be quite dead in ten seconds."

"What . . . what . . ."

"Back up, get in the car!"

He walked on trembling legs backward across the sidewalk. He heard a car door open, and then he was shoved.

Another pair of hands, also feminine but very strong, grasped him by the shoulders and pulled him into the back seat. The knife wielder moved in behind him, the door slammed, and the car lurched forward.

The knife was still pressing against his side, and Porthal knew the flesh had been pierced because he could feel the blood saturating his shirt.

Porthal was indignant, angry, and frightened all at the same time. And although he had never considered himself a particularly brave man, he knew he had to do something, and quickly, before his position worsened.

"What do you want?"

"Only some information, *monsieur*," replied the voluptuous one, still holding the knife steady against him.

"I am only a businessman, I swear . . ."

"You are a dealer in stolen goods, and you are about to make a purchase that we are very interested in knowing about."

The streetlights bathed the woman's face. Porthal had been a student of people his whole life. He could read them, read the good and bad in their eyes.

It was the reason he had survived and prospered all these years.

In this woman's eyes, Myron Porthal saw death.

With all the power he could muster, he shook off the hands that held his shoulders, struck away the hand holding the knife to his chest, and lurched toward the door.

He barely felt the needle as it punctured the soft, flabby skin at the base of his neck. Seconds later, his head lolled in the woman's lap.

He could still smell her perfume.

FOURTEEN

The villa of Sedji Bon Ali Cadiz was nestled on a bluff overlooking the bright lights of Deauville, with the Hôtel du Golf on one side, more vast estates on the other side, and giant trees as a backdrop.

It was two stories with twelve rooms each, a swimming pool and tennis court in the rear, and a great room that a normal-size house would be lost in.

If it wasn't the choicest piece of property around, it was considered among the top ones by the beautiful, laughing people carrying their drinks with them from limousines to the villa's lush interior.

Carter and Serena were among them.

"Let's circulate, darling," she bubbled. "I haven't seen any of these people in ever so long!"

"Don't you think you ought to introduce me to the host?"

"Cadiz? Oh, darling, he never makes his appearance at these soirees until everyone's already roaring drunk or his current amour has arrived." Suddenly she spotted someone in a crowd across the room. "Clair, darling! Oh, excuse me, Nick," she purred, pecking Carter on the cheek. "It's Lady Bolton and I've *got* to hear all the dirt about the divorce."

"Serena . . ." He grasped her arm gently but firmly.

"Yes?"

"Don't forget why we're here."

She threw him a dazzling smile. "Darling, for a million dollars, I forget nothing. And I have a lot better things than mere gossip to discuss with some of these wealthy matrons. You will see!"

She glided across the room, and Carter took stock.

Evidently, he mused, Sedji Cadiz liked a vast cross section of people for his amusement. There were the ultrarich, the very rich, the near rich, and the hangers-on. The latter were mostly titled aristocrats with frayed cuffs, alcohol-fogged eyes, and were termed by the others as "been rich," even if they hadn't.

Serena had given him a detailed description of the gem broker, Myron Porthal. He was nowhere to be seen, and as far as "shady characters of Serena's type," he saw very few. But then, on this level, he was pretty sure that even the crooks would be classy and circumspect.

"A drink, sir?"

The girl was a picture of calm dignity. She was dark, with beautiful eyes that remained passive as Carter's bored into them. He glanced over the servant girl's shoulder at the milling throng. He couldn't help comparing the overdressed, overly made-up, overbearing women in the room to the purity of this girl's Spanish face and form.

The servant girl definitely came out on top.

"*Monsieur?*"

"What? . . . Oh, yes." The tray was a mishmash of fruit-laden glasses and frozen daiquiris. In the mess he found a glass of wine and winked his thanks.

The girl gave him a whisper of a smile and glided away. The straightness of her back and the movement of her hips and buttocks—even in the ill-fitting uniform skirt—made men turn in her wake.

Carter moved onto the veranda.

The villa was high enough so that the entire part of Le Havre across the bay could be seen. Directly below, Deauville stretched like a posh velvet blanket to the beach.

The sounds of the party in the room behind him grew and spewed out onto the veranda. Suddenly the Killmaster found himself in the middle of a group containing a holy man of no definitive theology, a Princess Rasmine of Rome who sported a mile of cleavage, a man named Burton formerly of Wall Street U.S.A., and a wiry Spaniard who didn't take his eyes off Carter for a second.

It didn't take Carter long to size up the whole group, except for the Spaniard who called himself Ajeyo.

The princess's speech lapsed with each swallow of her drink. Before long, the accent was pure Brooklyn. Carter also learned that the financier, Burton, was now traveling under another name on a Costa Rican passport and was very much in demand in the United States for questioning by the Securities and Exchange Commission.

The holy man beamed at Carter and gave him, in careful English, his profoundest thoughts on humanity, on the direction the world was headed, and on the deplorable sexual freedom among the youth of the West.

All the while he was delivering his diatribe, he was benignly patting Princess Rasmine's shapely bottom.

During all this, the suave little Spaniard had slipped away. Carter saw him in a bent-headed exchange with Serena just inside the big room. When their chat ended, the woman looked up and summoned him with her eyes.

Carter excused himself from the group and made his way to her.

"You've been recognized," she chuckled.

"As what and by whom?"

"As one of us. It's that awful hard-eyed stare you have. You met Ajeyo?"

"Yes. I don't think he liked me."

"Not that at all. He just wanted to know what your specialty was."

"And you told him?"

"That you were a buyer in from Amsterdam with lots of money to spend."

"And that interested him?"

"Of course it did," she replied, her eyes darting around the room. "Ajeyo Montegro is the finest cat burglar on the Riviera. Within an hour, every crook and fence in the room will know you."

"Including Myron Porthal?"

"Let's hope," she replied, her eyebrows knitting.

"What is it?"

"Porthal isn't here. That's not like him. He usually comes very early, socially does his business, and leaves early. Being this late is not like him."

A frown creased Carter's forehead as well. "Damn. Perhaps they are making the trade tonight."

"No. Lady Bolton and the other buyers I know have told me that Monsieur Porthal wouldn't be getting the goods he has been describing until tomorrow. Hello, what's this . . . ?"

Carter followed her stare to the large double doors leading into the room. A man and a woman were just entering the room, arm in arm, like royalty. They both radiated the aristocratic characteristics of wealth and composure.

The man was small, with jet-black hair and a dark complexion. There was a sharp, unfinished appearance to his face and a hungry look in his dark eyes and thin mouth. He seemed to move casually yet carefully, as though he were walking on eggs.

"Cadiz?" Carter said.

"One and the same."

"He looks like a mongoose at a cobra farm," Carter commented dryly.

"That's why he's so rich, darling. But listen to the tongues wag about the woman on his arm."

Carter's eyes shifted. The woman was strikingly beautiful in a dark green lamé dress that hugged her long figure like a shimmering emerald skin. The short matching jacket failed to hide the thrust of her small, braless breasts in the low-cut bodice.

But it was her face, beneath blue-black hair swept back into a tight roll, that was most striking.

"Do you know her?" he murmured.

Serena nodded. "It's my business to know rich people, Nick. How can you rob the rich if you don't know who they are? She is—or was—a top model in England. Comes from a fine, old, wealthy family. I imagine that's where she met Sedji. He likes to collect wealthy young debs. Her name is Marta Penn."

Carter listened, but he had already dismissed both people. This night he was only interested in thieves.

He checked his watch. "It's getting late."

"These things take time, Nick. Patience. Circulate, we might get a bite yet. I'm going to pay my respects to our host."

Carter circulated, growing more agitated by the minute. At the end of an hour, he was disgusted and not a single soul had approached him.

He also noted that Myron Porthal had not shown, which made him even more nervous.

He meandered away from the party and found himself in the study, which was more like a religious museum. The walls and ceiling were hung with Christian and Moslem artifacts going clear back to the Crusades.

He moved along the glass cases, each one lighted to show the treasure inside. There were swords with jeweled hilts, statues, crucifixes of stone, wood, and ivory, and a fairly complete set of gold and silver plate that looked ancient.

"So here you are!"

It was Serena. So intent had Carter been on the items in the case before him that he hadn't heard her enter the room.

"Quite a collection, isn't it? Sedji has been gathering this stuff for years."

Carter forgot the collection and moved to meet her as she approached. "Anything?"

"*Nada*," she replied, "but we've got the word out. Something could come up before morning."

"Porthal?"

"No sign," she said, fitting a cigarette into a holder.

Carter lit hers and one of his own. "How well do you know him?"

"Well enough. Why?" she asked, pursing her lips to blow out a long plume of smoke.

"Know where he lives?"

"Yes."

"Then I think we should push a little. I want to go see him."

Serena shrugged. "He'll deny everything, probably tell us nothing."

Carter smiled. "Serena, you know there are ways to persuade people to cooperate."

"Yes, Nick . . . and I know you know them all."

"Let's go!"

He took her by the arm and they left the room. Skirting the crowded great room, they were making for the front door when Serena spoke again.

"You know, Nick, it would help a lot if I had some idea of what we're looking for. I know there must be something special in what this gang lifted."

"There is."

"You'd be smart telling me."

His hesitation was brief. "Okay, why not. It's a statue, probably small, of a Madonna and Child. It's probably a lot like one of those that Cadiz has in his cases back there."

Suddenly Serena stopped, her hand grasping his forearm in a viselike grip.

"An icon? . . . Of the Madonna and Child? . . . Made of ivory, gold, encrusted with stones, and elaborately carved?"

"Something like that, yes."

He knew from the sudden paleness of her face and the flash of her eyes that she had something.

"Earlier tonight, Marta Penn showed Sedji a sketch of just such a statue. She wants to sell it to him. He happened to mention it to me."

"The London debutante?" Carter said incredulously.

"The ex-deb, ex-model. I told you the tongues would wag. Evidently she lost all her money several years ago. Since then, she has lived pretty well, mostly off men. I guess the statue could be an old family heirloom . . ."

"Or it could be that Marta has a new way of making a living." There was excitement in Carter's voice as he grasped her shoulders. "Where is she now? Is she still in the villa?"

"No, she left about a half hour ago. She told Sedji she had other plans for the evening."

"*Merde*," Carter grumbled. "Did he tell her he would buy the statue?"

"He told her he would take a look at it."

"When?"

"I don't know."

"C'mon!" Carter said, grasping her by the wrist and dragging her back toward the great room.

"Where?"

"To find Cadiz. We're going to have a little in-depth discussion!"

FIFTEEN

Pierre Donet took a sip of his Dubonnet and studied the stunning girl over the rim of his glass. She had come back to Robère's just as she said she would.

They were now on their second drink, and the chitchat-small talk was over.

This was dangerous. With the exchange coming off the next day, Donet would have to be alert and in top form. But he couldn't turn this down. The woman was too beautiful and too exciting.

Her name was Nanette. He hadn't asked her what her last name was. He didn't care.

"Would you like to dance?" he asked.

It was always Donet's closing gambit. The closeness of dancing always answered the final question without verbalizing it.

"I would." She smiled dazzlingly.

"You dance beautifully," he whispered a few moments later, holding her tightly enough to melt any ice remaining between them.

"So do you, Pierre," she replied. "It must be fascinating to live and work in a place like Deauville."

"It has its moments . . . especially when I meet someone as lovely as you."

They danced and chatted. Gradually he tightened his grip, pulling her into him.

She responded.

The music grew resonant and mellower, the lead guitar breaking into soft, romantic chords.

Donet's hands gripped the small of her back. They moved in slow, rhythmic time to the music, their bodies pressing in a provocative way against each other. She coursed her hands down over his sides under his jacket until they found his hips.

Easy, Donet thought, *so easy*. She was seducing him more than he was seducing her.

Her eyes were closed. She responded to the soft, sensuous rhythm of the music by grinding her pelvis against his groin.

And then her eyes suddenly lifted to meet his in a direct gaze, and her lips parted, her tongue flickering over their red sheen.

"I am renting a beach house in Benerville, on the Avenue Foch," she breathed.

Donet smiled. "My car is right outside."

Eager, Donet thought as her heels beat a fast tattoo on the sidewalk ahead of him, *she is ready and eager*.

He dropped his hand to her knee as he sped away from the curb. She didn't move it, so he kept it there throughout the fifteen-minute ride to Deauville's western suburb.

In front of the house, he tried to kiss her, but she held him off. "Inside, Pierre, let us go inside. Hurry!"

She slid from the car and moved up the narrow walk, her hips moving smoothly under the tight-fitting dress she wore.

Perhaps it was the way she moved, or the scent of her that wafted back to invade his nostrils. But whatever it was, Pierre Donet did not see the man and the other woman standing just inside the door.

Only the sound of a footstep alerted him to their presence.

"What the hell is this?" he cried out as they moved toward him.

He started to turn back toward his conquest of the evening, when he heard, rather than felt, the stunning blow behind his right ear. He staggered, but before he became completely aware of the pain from the first blow, a second landed, and he sank to the floor, unconscious.

Julian Carmont paid off the cab two blocks from his building and waited until the puzzled driver was out of sight before walking the rest of the distance.

The taxi driver would wonder at his fare's odd request but would probably forget it by morning. The wealthy tourists did strange things when they were on vacation in a place like Deauville.

Julian had driven the rented Citroën up the mountain and around the perimeter of the golf course, with the cab right behind him. He had finally parked and locked the car in a small lane about two hundred yards from the fifth tee, and then took the cab back to the center of Deauville.

It would be a simple maneuver to walk directly to the car off the fifth tee. He would then dump the bag and clubs in the trunk and, without a backward look, drive to Paris.

By tomorrow evening he would be in Lisbon, where new identity papers and a new passport had already been purchased. The following morning he would fly to Rio.

The door of his apartment had barely shut behind him when the telephone started ringing. Carmont's first thought was to ignore it, but then he remembered telling Carmine to check with him one last time before he sailed.

"Yes?"

"Monsieur Carmont? . . . Monsieur Julian Carmont?"

The voice was low and husky without being sexy, and the words were spoken with an odd accent that Julian couldn't place.

"Yes, who is this?"

"My name doesn't matter."

"Listen, it is very late. . ."

"Shut up, Julian Carmont, and listen to what I have to say. A few weeks ago, you masterminded a robbery of the Ritz Hôtel in Paris. The people who committed this robbery with you were Marta Penn, Dino Foche, Claudia Biget, Carmine Fragunet, Alain Mittain, and Monsieur Pierre Donet—''

''Who the hell are you?'' Carmont gasped, interrupting the roll call he knew so well.

''Monsieur Donet is currently our guest. We learned of him through the gem dealer, Myron Porthal.''

As the voice droned on, detailing every move of the robbery, right down to the method of exchanging the gems for cash the following day, Carmont's blood ran colder. At the same time, sweat popped out in the small of his back and beaded up on his forehead.

''. . . and lastly, Monsieur Carmont, we know that the loot from the robbery is hidden somewhere on a boat named the *Marionette* in Honfleur harbor.''

''Why are you doing this?''

''It is very simple, Monsieur Carmont. You have stolen something that belongs to us. We want it back.''

Carmont's mind had calmed even if his body hadn't. This woman wasn't the police, that was obvious. She probably wasn't alone, either. No one person, especially a woman, could take Pierre Donet.

''Are you prepared to pay for it?'' Carmont managed to reply, surprised at the calm in his voice.

''Don't be foolish, *monsieur*. We have no intention of paying for our own property.''

''Then you can go to hell.''

There was a short pause before the woman spoke again. ''You are taking this much too lightly, *monsieur*. Where are you now?''

''In my apartment, of course.''

''I mean, where are you in your apartment?''

''The living room . . . why?''

''Go into the bedroom, *monsieur,* and then come back and tell me what you have found.''

''Look, I—''

''Go! Now!''

Angrily, Carmont dropped the phone and stalked across

the long, narrow room to his bedroom. He whipped open the door, switched on the light, and immediately staggered back against the wall.

Myron Porthal lay on his bed. A leather garrotte was cinched tightly around his neck. Carmont didn't need to approach or touch the body. From the open, bulging eyes and the chalky color of the man's face, Carmont knew he was dead.

He switched the light off and staggered back to the phone on shaky feet.

"I'm here."

"Good," the woman replied. "You now know that we will stop at nothing to retrieve our property."

"What do you want?" Carmont said, not attempting to hide the acquiescence in his voice.

"Better, much better, *monsieur*. You are now being sensible. We could, of course, merely board the *Marionette* and take what we want. But that might become messy, and very noisy. Also, we are interested in only one article that you stole. Once we have that back, you may dispose of the rest of your ill-gotten gains as you see fit."

Carmont's heart leaped in his chest. It wouldn't be a total loss after all.

"Do you agree, *monsieur*?"

"Of course," Carmont replied quickly, his brain going one hundred miles an hour, trying to figure out what single item in all the loot could possibly be worth all this trouble. "What is it you want?"

"There was a small icon . . . a Madonna and Child."

Carmont almost fainted with relief. The Madonna! They wanted that damned Madonna, and all he was going to do was throw it in the sea!

"Are you still there, *monsieur*?"

"Yes, yes, I am still here. I know the Madonna, and we have it."

"Excellent. I assume you will be willing to give it up if we give you our word that we will cause you no more trouble?"

"Yes, yes, of course."

"Then go to Honfleur, now. Board your boat and leave the harbor as soon as the tide is up."

"Yes."

"Bear left along the Côte de Grace. Do you know the old German fortifications on the hill above Cricqueboeuf?"

"Yes, I know them."

"And the cove just below them?"

"Yes."

"Pull into that cove. Leave your boat, with the Madonna, and climb the rocks above the beach. There are three concrete bunkers in the pasture above the beach. Go into the top bunker and leave the Madonna. Return to your boat, but don't leave until a signal is given from the bunker. The signal will be a flash . . . two short, two long, one short. Do you understand all that, *monsieur*?"

"Yes."

"Good. Leave your apartment at once, Monsieur Carmont. And, remember, we will be watching you at all times. *Au revoir*."

Carmont replaced the receiver and rolled in a sailor's tottering swagger to the bar. He poured a quarter of a glass of scotch, downed it, and poured another. When half of that was gone, he found that he could breathe evenly again.

"The Madonna," he said aloud to his own white-faced image in the bar's back mirror. "All they want is that damned Madonna."

Why they wanted it was of no concern to Julian Carmont. The fact that they were ruthless, and would go to any lengths to get it, was.

And he could keep the rest of the gems. *That* was what was important to Julian Carmont.

Oh, he would have to alter his plans now, find a new fence.

But that was easily enough done. Julian Carmont knew fences all over the world.

As he let himself out of the apartment, his agile mind was

already devising an alternate plan, a plan that he would put into effect right away.

In fact, the moment after he delivered the accursed Madonna at Cricqueboeuf.

Marta Penn swung up through the hatch and moved across the narrow deck to a ladder that led up to the pier.

Dino Foche was asleep below. Carmine sat in the bow, smoking.

"I'm going over to Tabori's bakery. There should be someone there by now, even if they aren't open yet. I'll get us some croissants and coffee."

Carmine Fragunet nodded. "Don't be too long. Tide's coming in fast. We'll be able to leave soon."

"Only a few minutes."

Marta waved over her shoulder and moved along the brick walkway above the Honfleur quay, a lone figure all in white against the false dawn sifting over the unbroken line of five- and six-story buildings that surrounded the water on three sides.

She was wearing white jeans, sneakers, a white denim jacket, and under the jacket, a T-shirt. Only the bottom two buttons of the jacket were fastened, to hide the bulge the Madonna made under the shirt and her belt.

Carmine hadn't noticed her remove the Madonna from the black rubber oar casing and slip it into her jeans. The brooch with the fake gems, the string of pearls, and three bricks for weight were still in the casing.

"I think I'll dump these in the harbor now," she had told him. "I might forget at sea."

Carmine had shrugged. If Julian Carmont was the boss, Marta was the second boss. What they did meant little to him. All he wanted was his split, and as quickly as possible. Keeping Dino Foche sober was getting to be a chore, and Carmine had a woman waiting for him in Morocco with breasts the size of cantaloupes.

Marta turned left over the bridge at the end of the quay, toward a bar-restaurant sign marked Tabori in faded gold letters against a white peeling background.

Below her to the left, lights were starting to blink on in some of the sport fishing boats. A half hour from now, there would be a long line of them circling in the center of the small harbor, waiting for the drawbridge to be lifted for their exit.

"Bonjour, mademoiselle."

The voice startled Marta. It belonged to a tall, broad-shouldered man in a pair of tattered jeans and a paint-splattered sweatshirt. Tufts of bright blond hair curled from under a woolen seaman's cap.

"Bonjour, monsieur . . ."

"It will be a perfect morning to capture the sunrise."

Then she saw the easel and an array of paints and a palette set out on an old crate.

For a moment, the intensity of his stare gave her pause. Then his boyish face broke into a broad smile, and she sighed.

"You startled me. I didn't see you against the buildings."

"Ah, pardon, mademoiselle."

Marta moved on, dismissing him from her thoughts. In an hour, the area around the quay would be full of artists preparing to hawk their work to the tourists. This man was only one of many.

She walked to the end of the block and turned into the alley behind the restaurant. The lights were on in the bakery attached to the restaurant. Through the window, she saw the dark head with the long, knotted pigtail darting to and fro.

He answered her knock at once.

"Ah, bonjour, mademoiselle. I was not sure you were coming after all," he said in his singsong French.

"I told you I might be a little late," Marta replied, opening her jacket and pulling out the Madonna wrapped in a chamois sack. "Can you do it?"

"Of course." He laughed, taking it from her. "It is even smaller than you said. It will bake easily into a loaf."

"And you're sure it won't be harmed?"

"*Absolument, mademoiselle*," he cackled. "I must say it is an odd way of giving someone a present."

"I have odd friends."

He shrugged. "And now, *mademoiselle*, the price we agreed upon?"

From her pocket Marta extracted a thousand-franc note. "One hundred and twenty-five dollars is a lot of money for five loaves of bread. See that you do a good job."

The money disappeared beneath his apron. "Don't forget this includes delivery." He cackled again.

"Room four-twelve, Hôtel du Golf, remember?"

"Of course. It will be no problem. I am through here by eleven, and I live in Trouville. I will drop them off on my way home."

"Good," Marta replied, unable to suppress a sigh of relief. "Does that thousand francs include three cups of coffee and a half-dozen croissants to go?"

"It's a pleasure!" he cackled, scurrying toward a tray of freshly baked croissants in a rack against a far wall.

Five minutes later, Marta was hurrying down the side of the quay toward the boat. She was almost there, when a taxi rocked to a halt beside her and discharged a very nervous Julian Carmont.

SIXTEEN

Carter had rented the little Renault 5 compact when he and Tamara had first arrived in Deauville. His thinking then had been the inconspicuousness of the little car among so many just like it.

Now, as he hit the D513 coastal route between Deauville and Honfleur, he wished he had been thinking more about speed than inconspicuousness.

"Uh, Nick . . ." said a white-faced Serena from the opposite seat, her knees braced against the dash and her voluptuous body straining against the seat belt on every curve.

"Yeah?"

"Do you know this road?"

"Yeah."

"Then you know it curves like a scared snake."

"Yeah."

"Then, goddamnit, slow down! You're scaring the hell out of me!"

"Close your eyes," he hissed, throwing the Renault into third and hurtling around a lumbering truck.

He barely swerved back into the lane when a climbing S-curve came up. Keeping the car in third, he took all four curves on two wheels, and planted the accelerator back to the floor when he hit fourth gear again on a straightaway.

"Want to tell me who this Yuri Androssov guy is?" she said in a quaking voice.

"You might as well know. He's a transplanted Russian attached to a Bulgarian hit squad."

"Then *they* are in on this?"

"You knew it already," he growled, grinding the little car around another curve and straining his eyes at a road sign: Honfleur 4 km.

"I only heard rumors. Damn you, you're going to kill us both!"

Dawn was coming on fast. To their left across the bay, it was starting to bleed out the twinkling lights of Le Havre. To their right, the gray light was washing over the pastoral Norman countryside.

How peaceful it was, Carter thought, with its quaint, thatched-roof cottages, its goats and sheep and its cattle lowing gently for their morning feed and milking.

He hoped it would stay that way, but he doubted it.

They had learned from Cadiz that Marta Penn would bring the Madonna to him the next evening around six for his perusal. From the sketch she had shown him, and her description of it, Cadiz had told her that it might well be worth over a half-million francs.

A hundred thousand dollars, at the current exchange rate, wasn't a fortune, but it was probably enough to make her keep the appointment.

But Carter couldn't take that chance. He and Serena had paid a call on Myron Porthal. The housekeeper had been frantic. Monsieur Porthal had not arrived home at his usual time from the shop. Not only that, Monsieur Porthal had not even called. He always called. And he had missed a party at Monsieur Cadiz's villa that he had been looking forward to for days.

It was strange, very strange, the lady thought.

Not to the Killmaster. It smelled. Androssov and Company could well have gotten to the gem dealer. If they had,

Carter was fairly sure that by now he was full of the same dope Koenigburger had been given in Paris.

Porthal would sing like a nightingale, and depending on how much he knew, the crew from the opposite side would be many steps closer to the Madonna than Carter and the good guys.

How many steps, it was impossible to tell, but too many to wait for Marta Penn to arrive at Cadiz's that evening.

Also, there was always the chance—slim, Carter guessed—that Marta Penn was legit and the Madonna she wanted to sell to her old lover really was a family heirloom.

He felt even more uneasy after a phone call to Paris.

"This is Carter. Give me Weatherby."

Two minutes later, a groggy voice came on the line. "God, I've been trying to raise you at your hotel for the last hour!"

"What's up?" Carter asked, the old familiar warnings going up his spine.

"Yuri Androssov. He chartered a single-engine out of Bayeaux."

"You lost him," Carter said flatly.

"Not there. My boys had to scrounge like hell to get their own charter, *and* pay an arm and a leg to bribe a controller for Androssov's flight plan."

"Where to?"

"Le Havre. They landed about ten minutes before he did, and waited. He cabbed to Pont de Tancarville. That's up the Seine a way from the place it flows out into the bay and the ocean."

"I know," Carter said, gnashing his teeth with impatience. "What then?"

"He ate, drank, and walked around. He just walked around until after dark. Then the son of a bitch went down to a marina just above the bridge and calmly stole a power launch."

"He what?"

"That's right. He hot-wired a big launch and just sailed off with it downriver. The boys watched him through binoculars. There was nothing they could do. That's where they lost him."

"Shit."

"My sentiments exactly."

"He could have gone anywhere."

"Sorry, pal. What now?" Weatherby sighed.

"I'll stay on it from this end. What about the two who made contact with Androssov in Bayeaux?"

"They're holed up in Deauville. We have poeple on them, but if they've contacted anyone, it's been done by phone."

"Later," Carter said, and headed back for the car and Serena.

Normandy covered a vast area, including the countylike *départements* of Eure and Calvados. In the beginning, Deauville had merely been a jumping-off spot to start looking, because of Serena's connections. But now it looked like the Deauville area was the jackpot.

Carter dropped by the hotel and checked to see if Tamara had clocked in from her perch on the cathedral roof across from Dino Foche's boat in Honfleur.

She had, leaving messages every hour for the last six hours. The first five were nothing: *All quiet.*

The sixth, taken by the hotel switchboard operator fifteen minutes before, was dynamite: *Our Bulgarian friend is on the scene. Two gentlemen still on boat, now joined by woman. Looks as though they might be getting ready to sail. Suggest you get here right away.*

They hit the city limits on the ocean side, and Carter throttled the Renault down to forty. Two turns brought him to the drawbridge over the quay.

There was already quite a bit of activity in the harbor, and he could see the bridgemaster unlocking his controls.

Two blocks further, Carter cut away from the main street into a smaller one. One more block, and he hung a right into a cobblestone alley and slammed to a halt.

"What's this?"

"It used to be a cathedral a few centuries ago," Carter replied, sliding from the car. "Now it's a maritime museum. With a very accessible roof. Stay here!"

He darted into the shadows and felt along the wall until his fingers found the wooden ladder. At one time it had been used by the bell ringer to get to the outside belfry. Now it was kept in repair so maintenance people could have easy access to the roof.

It took less than a minute to make the climb and drop to the sloping area of the roof.

"Tamara?" he whispered.

"Here, in front of the belfry. Come slowly, you'll frighten the pigeons!"

Carter went into a crouch until the slant was too much to handle, and then he dropped to his belly. He crab walked around the belfry and rolled into the little area where Tamara lay.

"God, I thought you were never going to pick up my messages."

"It sounds as though you've got some activity."

"Lots. Here!"

He took the glasses from her hands and fitted them to his eyes. "Talk to me."

"The two men on the boat had a big argument earlier. One of them threw a bottle of whiskey overboard."

"One of them, Dino Foche, is a drunk," Carter said, nodding. "They're probably trying to keep him sober. Go on!"

"A woman came aboard about an hour ago."

"Describe her."

Carter stayed silent through the description. By the end of it, he was smiling broadly beneath the glasses.

"Something?" Tamara asked.

"Her name is Marta Penn." Quickly he explained the offer the woman had made to Sedji Cadiz the previous evening.

"Do you think the Madonna is on the boat?"

"My thinking is leaning more and more that way, yes. Anything else?"

"Everything was quiet for a while, then the woman left. She went over there, to that bakery behind the restaurant. She's still there. Oh, wait a second . . ."

"What?"

"Just before she went to the bakery, she threw something overboard into the harbor. It was a bag of some kind, black. It looked like it was made out of rubber."

Carter made a mental note and started shifting the glasses. "Where's Androssov?"

"There, sitting at that easel by the bridge. The woman talked to him when she passed."

"Friendly?"

"No, I don't think she knew him. I would never have noticed or recognized him myself if he hadn't bent over and picked up a brush he dropped. His cap got caught on the easel and came off for a few seconds. I would know that hair in a minute. Look . . ."

"What?"

"That's the woman, isn't it?"

Carter found the image in white, centered on her face, and adjusted the glasses.

It was Marta Penn.

"What's she carrying?"

"Food, it looks like," Carter replied. "Probably coffee, the carton is steaming."

He followed her progress across the bridge and down the quay.

Just as she got abreast of the boat, a cab pulled up and a tall man, agitation in his manner and worry written all over his face, grasped Marta Penn's arm so hard that the carton flew from her grasp.

Marta had never seen Julian Carmont like this. He was

always cool and calm, always in control. But now he was like a wild man.

He stepped on deck right behind her, then brushed quickly by her toward the hatch.

"Carmine!"

"Yeah" came the reply from the bow.

"Rig sail and start the engine! I want to be first in line when the bridge goes up!"

Wordlessly, Carmine started unrolling the sail wrap. Evidently, the plan was changed. Originally, Carmont was going to pick up the goods from the hotel. Now he was on the boat.

If the change puzzled Carmine, it didn't bother him. Nothing bothered Carmine. All he wanted to do was collect his money and get to Cantaloupe Breasts in Casablanca.

But Carmont's presence did bother Marta. "Julian, what the hell is wrong with you?"

He didn't reply, didn't even glance over his shoulder, as he dropped through the hatch into the cabin.

"Dino!"

"Yeah, yeah, what the hell is it?" came the groggy reply. "Julian . . . ?"

"Get your ass topside and help Carmine with the sail."

"Mon Dieu, Julian, what the hell are you doing here?"

"Never mind, move your ass!" Carmont thundered.

"All right, all right." Dino Foche lurched from the cabin, practically crashing into Marta. "What devil got into him?"

"I don't know. Do as he says."

"Yeah, yeah."

Marta dropped through the hatch. Carmont had already pushed the table aside and was moving through the deck hatch into the bilge.

"Julian . . ."

There was no answer. Below, she could hear the clatter and a few mumbled curses as he went through the suitcase containing the loot.

Then half his body was back above the deck. His face was bloodred and his eyes were swollen. They stared at her like those of some trapped animal.

"Where is it?"

"Where is what?"

"The Madonna!" he cried, his voice almost a squeak. "Where is the damned thing?"

"Julian, what's wrong with you?"

"Tell me!" he practically screamed, leaping from the hole in the deck and crouching in front of her.

"What difference does it make? You told me to get rid of it."

"At sea . . . I told you to get rid of it *at sea*!"

She hesitated, her mind whirling. She had no idea what had set him off, but set off he definitely was, and with murder in his eye.

She started backing toward the hatch when he came for her like a leaping cat.

For a second she thought he was going to hit her. Anger flared his nostrils, his chest heaved, and if possible, his eyes grew even wider.

Instead, he grasped both her wrists, spun with her, and sent her crashing against the opposite bulkhead.

"Julian, you son of a . . ."

"Where the hell is it? I told you to dump it at sea!"

"Sea, harbor . . . what's the goddamned difference?"

He came for her again, his raised hands aiming for her throat.

Marta grabbed the closest thing at hand, her heavy purse from the bunk. She grasped it by the bottom and whipped him with the sharp shoulder chain.

It struck him across the nose and then on the forehead, leaving a deep gash that spilled blood into his eyes.

"You bitch!" he snarled, tearing the purse from her hands and closing his fingers over her wrists. He wrestled her arms behind her back.

Marta struggled against him wildly, ripping his shirt when she lunged to bite his shoulder. Her sharp-toed shoes gouged his shins, and one knee lifted in an effort to reach his crotch.

Together, they slammed into the bulkhead and rocked away again. Low growls erupted from both their throats, and beads of perspiration stood out on their faces as they struggled.

In desperation, Carmont forced her toward the bunk, trying to push her down into it. His feet tangled with hers, and she fell back. He tripped, but somehow Marta managed to flip both their bodies so that she fell heavily on top of him.

He cried out in agony as his spine cracked against the edge of the bunk. The cry soon turned to an animallike growl of fury as he managed to lace his fingers around her throat.

With pain shooting clear up to the top of his head, he managed to roll her over and cover her with his heavier body.

"Julian . . ." she gagged, writhing beneath his weight, throwing her head from side to side, her teeth clenched.

"Where is it, bitch? What have you done with it?"

"In the harbor . . . I threw it in the harbor!"

"You're lying, you've got to be!"

"I'm not! Julian, you're killing me! I . . . can't . . . breathe . . ."

"Goddamn you, I will kill you if you don't tell me what you've done with it. I know you, you bitch. I can read you like a book."

"No!" she protested again, gasping for breath. There was a red film starting to form before her eyes, and the ceiling above her started to swim.

Suddenly, mustering all the strength in her tall, lithe body, she heaved upward with her hips. At the same time, she clenched both hands into a single fist and brought it, twice, down across the bridge of his nose.

Again Carmont cried out and he momentarily loosened his hold. Marta was able to writhe from beneath him. She lurched toward the hatch, with Carmont right behind her. He managed to entwine his fingers in the back of her jacket, but she quickly shrugged out of it. In so doing, she was turned backward toward the hatch.

"Stop, Julian!" she cried, backpedaling as fast as her feet would take her.

Too late, she remembered the open hole in the deck leading to the bilges. She felt only air beneath her feet. She tried to twist to the side, but it was too late. Her forward momentum was too much. She went into the hatch, and then her knees struck the sharp edge on the opposite side of the hole.

The crack of her bones was like two rifle shots in the confined cabin. Marta screamed with the pain, and then her momentum carried her on across the deck.

Her flight ended with a sickening crunch as her head collided with the edge of a massive sea chest.

Julian Carmont lay where he fell, stunned, as he looked across at her crushed skull. Then, through the blood in his eyes, he saw Carmine bending over her.

"Jesus Christ, Julian, are you nuts?"

"What?" Carmont gasped, digging his fingers into his eyes. "What . . . ?"

"She's dead," Carmine replied.

SEVENTEEN

"What was that?"

Carter flicked his eyes to meet Tamara's. He didn't comment. There was no need. They both knew it had been a woman's scream.

He darted the glasses around to the other boats, where preparations for a morning sail were being made. A few faces registered that they, too, had heard the scream, but no one moved to investigate.

In minutes, work was resumed and the harbor continued to come alive.

"They're moving!" Tamara said.

"I see."

The *Marionette* was easing from her berth. In no time, she was in the center of the harbor and circling for a run at the bridge. Again, Carter shifted the glasses, this time to the bridgemaster at his controls.

Levers were pulled, silent hydraulics were engaged, and the traffic barricades at each end of the bridge started to descend.

"What are we going to do?" Tamara whispered anxiously beside him. "Androssov's people have obviously made some kind of contact. Aren't we going to follow them?"

"Yes, eventually," Carter growled. "As soon as we find

out what Androssov does. And that's happening right now . . .''

The Bulgarian had already packed up his easel and paints. He was now walking leisurely along the quay toward the rising drawbridge. He passed the bridge and the road, and entered a parking lot adjacent to the outside marina.

At first Carter thought that the man was heading for a car. But he went on through the parking lot and descended some stone steps into the marina.

And then Carter remembered the stolen power launch. He raked the glasses over the white sterns of several boats, and found the one he wanted minutes before Androssov dropped to its deck.

All boats and ships have their name and home port on the stern. This one didn't. Androssov had slashed across it with a paintbrush. The stern was solid white, with no markings.

"The *Marionette* is through the lock!"

Carter nodded behind the glasses. "And there goes Androssov to follow. I guess that pretty well answers one question. Let's go!"

They ran, crouched, across the roof, and Tamara led the way down the ladder. In the alley, Carter shoved a thick sheaf of bills into her hand and jogged her around the maritime museum to the quay.

"What's this for?"

"Make a run down the boats. One of them will have a diver aboard with scuba gear. Offer him that whole wad if you must, to bring up that rubber bag. Do you remember where Marta tossed it?"

Tamara nodded. "About twenty, maybe twenty-five feet toward the center of the harbor from where the *Marionette* was berthed."

"Then, if your diver is any good, it shouldn't take him over a half hour to retrieve it."

"You're going after them . . .''

It was in her eyes and the long face. After all this, she was not getting in on the kill.

"The Madonna might or might not be in that bag. If Marta Penn is double-crossing her buddies, it probably is, but we can't take a chance. We have to cover both ends. Now go!"

With a resigned shrug, Tamara moved out of the shadows and headed for the quay and a line of boats.

Carter retraced his steps to the car and an anxious Serena.

"What happened?"

The Killmaster gave her a quick rundown as he backed the Renault around. He headed for the main drag that would take them over the drawbridge and onto the beach road out of Honfleur.

"So we struck gold!"

"I think so, one way or the other."

"Is this Tamara woman one of yours?"

"No, she's a defecting Russian."

"Jesus, Nick, how can you be sure of her? Hell, if the Madonna *is* in this rubber bag, she could be long gone before you can get back here!"

"She's a safe bet," he replied grimly. "I've tested her."

"How?"

"I forced her into a bind and made her kill one of her own in a London hotel room."

Serena shuddered. "And they say that crooks are bad people."

Carter made a couple of lifelong French enemies by crowding into the line of cars waiting to cross the bridge. A precious fifteen minutes were lost waiting for the long line of boats to scoot through, and then the bridge started coming down.

Carter wasn't worried. The *Marionette* would only make about five knots under the power of its small engine. Even if they caught a good wind, it would only add four or five knots more to that.

He was fairly sure he knew where he could sight them.

The bridge was down and the barricades came up. Carter dropped the Renault into first and made a right turn over the bridge.

The road followed the inland waterway for about four

hundred yards and then veered to the left. In his mind, he visualized the waterway. It went past a long park to his right. Beyond the park was a beach, then long, craggy cliffs, and finally a point that jutted out into the ocean.

When he was sure they were abreast of the point, Carter cranked the wheel to the right. The road was barely more than a goat path, potted, narrow, and dusty. Twice he almost lost control when big rocks loomed up out of nowhere and he had to careen off into the sand to avoid them.

Finally they reached the very peak of the point, and Carter cut the engine. He clambered from the car, with Serena right behind him.

"Careful," he called over his shoulder, picking his way over the rocks. "The edge comes up quick, and it's a two-hundred-foot drop to the sea and the rocks below."

Serena held back a few feet until Carter came to a halt, and then she edged up behind him.

The drop was more like three hundred feet, but the view, even heavily laid over with morning mist, was spectacular.

Directly across the water, they could barely discern the squat white oil storage tanks lining the Canal du Havre. Beyond them, white smoke curled lazily into the mist from the stacks of the Renault plant.

Far to their right lay the Seine, emptying into the bay of Le Havre. To their left was the lower coast of Normandy and the English Channel.

Carter narrowed his eyes behind the glasses and scanned the mouth of the bay.

He found the *Marionette*'s tall white sail about bay center. Almost a mile and a half to the rear, he saw the tiny dot of Androssov's power launch idling along in pursuit.

Carter sighed with relief. At least for now, the Russian was not overtaking them. The Killmaster had already reasoned that they had put some kind of pressure on Marta Penn and the rest of the gang. The chances were that all they wanted was the Madonna.

Carter's fear here was that the exchange would take place

at sea or somewhere up the Normandy coast, where he
wouldn't have time to overtake them in Serena's boat, the
Gypsy.

"Can you spot them?" Serena asked. "I can't see a
damned thing through this mist."

"I've got them."

Even as he spoke, he saw the *Marionette*'s sail heel to port.
He breathed a second sigh of relief.

"They're turning south. How well do you know the coast
from here to Deauville?"

"Like the back of my hand," Serena chuckled. "It's a
smuggler's dream . . . lots of coves and inlets. That's why
the Germans fortified it so much."

"Give me a rundown, all the way."

"There's an inlet, there, near Vasouy, and another near
Pennedepie, but it's dangerous, rocks. About three kilomet-
ers beyond that, there are two coves at Cricqueboeuf, one on
each side of the old German bunkers. Next place is the harbor
at Villerville, where the *Gypsy* is anchored. Beyond that is a
natural marina at Hennequeville. From there on it's open
swimming beach through Trouville, Deauville, all the way to
Houlgate."

Carter digested this and kept the glasses on the *Marionette*
as she tacked south. Androssov had fallen even farther behind and was making no attempt to catch up.

"They're staying about a mile out but following the coast.
C'mon!"

Back in the car, Carter handed Serena the binoculars.
"Stay on him!"

The D513 hugged the Côte de Grace all the way from
Honfleur to Deauville. Now and then it would dart inland a
few hundred yards, but always less than a half mile later it
would bend back toward the sea.

Carter's palms were sweating on the wheel. The car was
crawling along at less than ten miles per hour to keep pace
with the *Marionette* at sea.

They passed Vasouy and came up on Pennedepie, with no

change in the *Marionette*'s direction.

"The launch is picking up knots!"

"Dammit," Carter hissed. Maybe they planned on an exchange at sea after all.

At least, he thought, he and Serena were much closer to Villerville and the *Gypsy*.

The road cut inland, and Carter gunned the Renault up to sixty. They hit the village of Cricqueboeuf, and his eyes scanned the many signs until he found the one he wanted: *La Plage*. The beach.

He whipped toward the right and the ocean. Once again, he had to leave the main road and go over a tractor path to reach the cliffs.

"There they are!" Serena exclaimed, passing the glasses over. "The *Marionette* is coming around to port again."

"And the launch is picking up speed. What do you think?"

"Bring the binoculars around, back there to the road. See it?"

"Yes."

"All right, follow the road south until, just to the right of it, you can see the old bunkers in a pasture."

"I can't find them," Carter said, irritated.

"That's because the roofs were planted with sea grass for camouflage. They're grown over. Try and spot the hunks of round and square brown against the green of the pasture grass."

He found them, three of them, in a sloping pasture that ran to the edge of a bluff over the sea.

The two lower bunkers were squat concrete structures with gaping mouths facing the sea. Years before, the muzzles of deadly 88s had protruded from those openings.

The third bunker, about ninety yards above the others, was round, much larger, and had a narrow observation slit for an opening. That, Carter guessed, would have been the command bunker for this part of the coast, and the sleeping quarters of the watch.

The pasture itself was about a half-mile wide, and without

Serena's explanation, he could see the two rocky coves on either side.

The *Marionette* was heading for the one to the south, and Androssov was making a beeline to the northern cove.

It was all guesswork, but Carter thought he could see the Russians' plan. The fast power launch would be their escape as soon as the Madonna was theirs.

In confirmation, he saw two figures climb the fence between the road and the pastures. As they moved toward the command bunker, it was impossible to discern faces, even figures.

But he was willing to bet anything that both of them were women.

Julian Carmont was at the wheel. Carmine and Dino Foche were dropping sail as they weaved through the jutting rocks and into the cove.

He was calm now. The first few minutes after the debacle in Honfleur harbor had been hell. But he had forced himself to think, think, think.

Carmine had confirmed that Marta had put the Madonna, the brooch, and the pearls in an oar casing and tossed them into the harbor. He had seen her do it. And if Carmine had seen her, then whoever had been watching them would have also seen it.

Carmont was counting on the fact that the woman on the phone hadn't lied when she said that he would be watched every step of the way.

He was counting on that, and on his own ability to bluff.

"Come around!" Carmine called from the bow.

Carmont reversed the engine and skillfully swung the wheel. The *Marionette* eased to port, scraped her side briefly against the sheer rocks, and then settled in.

"Drop anchor!" Carmont said and heard the splash almost before the words had left his mouth.

He was just finishing wrapping a chamois around his magnum, when Carmine and Dino came aft.

"We want to know what's going on, Julian."

"I told you. Porthal has backed off. We will have to sail to England. I know someone in Falmouth who will give us as good a price as Porthal."

Carmine Fragunet was not very bright, but he was sly. He didn't like what he was hearing.

"It stinks, Julian. Smuggling stones into Cornwall is too much of a risk. I don't like it."

"I don't give a damn what you like or don't like, Carmine. It has to be done. I'll be back soon. And by the time I return, I want Marta's body wrapped, weighted, and dumped."

Without another word, Carmont stepped from the *Marionette*'s deck to the rocks and started to climb.

Carter growled fast, explicit instructions to Serena and installed her back in the car.

"I'm going to make a heroine out of you, lady, with the insurance company and the *Sûreté*. Now move!"

He watched the car until it hit the paved road and turned right toward Villerville. Then he returned to the point and started the long descent to the beach.

It didn't take long. Goats had already provided a path.

Once on the beach, he followed the coast, over rocks, across sandy beaches, and over a couple of low bluffs.

Fifteen minutes after starting his descent, he found the mouth of the north cove. The launch was nosed in to a narrow strip of sand, with a ground anchor trailing into the rocks from the bow.

There was no sign of Androssov, but Carter sensed the man was there, somewhere.

The Killmaster stripped to his waist. He slipped Hugo between his teeth and wound Wilhelmina's shoulder rig around his neck. The last thing he did before slipping into the water was kick off his shoes.

Julian Carmont stepped over the rise and found himself in a

pasture, practically in the middle of a herd of cattle. One old bull eyed him, made a grunting sound, and moved away. Most of the cows followed.

He stood upright and checked his position. There was a bunker to his right, one to his left, and a third, larger one, at the top of the pasture directly in front of him.

Striding forward, he made no effort to be quiet. At the bunker, he glanced once through the slit and then moved on around it to the inland side and the entrance.

There was no door, just a shadowed tunnel. On each side there were rooms of concrete and steel where once German soldiers had slept between their watches. He moved on through the tunnel toward the light and the main observation deck, the magnum in its chamois bag held at his side.

"Hello . . . is anyone here?"

The barest scrape of a shoe on cement made him whirl.

She was tall, and even in the shadows he could see that her figure was spectacular and her face beautiful. She held a Beretta with both hands in front of her magnificent chest, its small muzzle unwavering.

"Place the Madonna there on the ledge, Monsieur Carmont, and move away from it, slowly."

He recognized the voice. "Where is Pierre Donet?"

"Dead. But I am sure that will make no difference to you, *monsieur*. One less to split with. Now do as you are told."

Carmont raised the bag, at the same time slipping his hand inside. "I no longer have the Madonna."

"What?"

Her body tensed. For a second, Carmont was sure she was going to fire. His own finger tensed on the trigger of the magnum.

"The woman, Marta Penn, disobeyed me. She discarded the Madonna in the harbor at Honfleur."

"Monsieur Carmont, I will shoot first your right knee. Then, if you persist, I will shoot your left."

"I swear! Did you have anyone watching us?"

"Yes."

"Then contact them. I am sure they saw her throw a black rubber oar casing into the harbor."

The woman hesitated, and then she spoke. "Sofia?"

"Yes?" came a female voice from the shadows of the tunnel behind the woman with the gun.

"Call Yuri on the hand radio."

Carmont sighed. There were two of them. He could drop the first one easily and then get the second by spraying into the tunnel. But only if he had to. He prayed that they would believe him.

"Yuri . . . Yuri, we are in the bunker. Are you in the cove? Over!"

Static screeched loudly in the enclosed space, and then a muffled man's voice came through. "I'm here. Over."

"Carmont says that the Madonna was thrown into the bay in a black rubber oar cover by the woman. Did you see it? Over."

"I saw her throw something like that in the harbor. Over."

"Good. Hold."

"We must be sure the Madonna was in the bag, *monsieur*," said the one with the Beretta.

"It was, I swear it!" Carmont gasped.

"We will go down to your boat and speak to Marta Penn."

"You can't. There was an accident. She's dead."

Indecision clouded the woman's eyes. She tilted her head and spoke to the woman behind her. "Sofia . . . ?"

"I believe him, but we can check the boat to make sure before we leave."

"Very well."

It was in her eyes and the tension Julian Carmont saw in her shoulders. She was going to kill him.

His finger was already squeezing the trigger of the magnum when two slugs from Eva Stalnik's silenced Beretta tore into his chest, driving him back against the concrete wall of the bunker.

The roar of the magnum was like the sound of a cannon the confined space. The high-grain shell tore into the wo man's left hip, spinning her into Sofia Dobroskov's arms.

"Eva . . . Eva!"

"Hit . . . hip . . . oh, God, it hurts . . ."

Sofia thought fast. Carmont was dead. Eva was bleeding badly. The rule was, she should finish Eva off and go on with the mission. But it would be bad to leave the body to be found with Carmont.

The woman cried out in agony as Sofia hoisted her to her shoulder.

"It's all right, Eva. I'll take you to Yuri, then Maurice, and I will search their boat to make sure."

Staggering under the larger woman's weight, Sofia Dobroskov moved out of the bunker and down across the pasture.

Carter eased himself quietly over the rail as the woman's voice came over the two-way radio Yuri Androssov held to his ear.

The Killmaster's stocking feet made no noise as he moved over the deck forward. But he could have made some noise. Androssov was absorbed in the radio conversation.

And so was Carter. It brought a silent sigh of relief to his lips. Carmont didn't have the Madonna. Marta Penn had thrown it into the Honfleur harbor.

He was three feet behind Androssov when the Bulgarian's instincts warned him. He lurched for the revolver on the deck beside him. But he never got to it.

Carter's stiletto went into his brain from just behind his right ear.

Androssov was almost exactly Carter's size. It took the Killmaster less than two minutes to strip the body and climb into the Russian's clothes.

Carmine Fragunet had had it up to his ears. It was time to get out.

He told Dino Foche as much, but the other man was in a state of total fear. He couldn't move or speak, even when Carmine pulled the revolver from his belt and held it to the man's quivering head.

"Move, Dino! Hoist the anchor. We're getting the hell out of here!"

"But . . . Julian . . ." Dino managed to stammer at last. "We have to wait for Julian."

"Screw Julian. We're getting out of here!"

"You're going nowhere until I say you are. Throw the gun over the side."

Carmine whirled at the sound of the voice, his thumb instinctively flipping the safety catch to "off." The man was a dark image against the morning sky, partially hidden among the rocks. The outline of a rifle could be seen in his arms.

"You heard me," the voice barked again. "Throw the gun—"

At that moment the morning stillness was broken by what sounded like a Howitzer going off in one of the bunkers on the bluff above.

Carmine didn't care where the sound came from, or for what reason. It was enough that, for an instant, it had distracted the man in the rocks. He raised his own gun and, point-blank, pumped three slugs into the man's chest.

Maurice folded soundlessly back into the craggy rocks and disappeared.

Carmine immediately whirled on Dino Foche.

"Now, you son of a bitch, hoist that anchor or I'll blow you to hell, too!"

The little man suddenly had springs in his legs, running toward the stern and the anchor winch.

Carter was on his feet instantly when the first shot echoed over the bluff. When the second two came, he started over the bow. He was just scrambling up the rocks, when he saw the two women approach, one carrying the other, fireman fashion, on her shoulder.

He backed off and regained the bow of the launch just a
they staggered to the beach.

"Yuri, Yuri! Eva has been shot! Give me a hand!"

Carter's face was shielded from the speaker's eyes by the
body she carried. He leaned over the bow and hoisted the
wounded woman to the deck. Paying no attention, Sofia
leaped to the deck herself, only to find the muzzle of a 9mm
Luger two inches from the bridge of her nose.

"I rather imagine you know who I am. Take your clothes
off."

"What?" she screamed in disbelief.

"I don't have time to search you, and the Madonna is small
enough to be hidden anywhere. Take your clothes off!"

"We don't have it. The fool woman threw it in the harbor
at Honfleur."

"I know she did," Carter replied. "Or at least hope she
did. Now take off your goddamned clothes!"

Sophia complied. "Where's Yuri?"

"Below. Dead," Carter replied, using his free hand to
search Eva's supine body. "Just like this one's going to be if
you don't get her to a doctor."

Satisfied, he motioned Sofia away from the pile of
clothes, and then patted them down. This done, he walked to
the bow and dropped easily to the beach.

"I imagine there's a trawler out there somewhere that you
were going to meet, right?"

She nodded, grim-faced, her eyes full of hate, her bare
breasts rising and falling with each deep breath of anger she
took.

"Then I'd advise you," he said, tossing the keys to the
launch up at her, "to get her out there as quickly as possible."

"You are a son of a bitch."

"Aren't we all?" Carter said, already crawling up the
rocks.

He jogged across the pasture, Wilhelmina still ready in his
right hand even though he was pretty sure the war was over.

Once through the cows, he turned downhill toward the

each. The sun was up over the horizon now, clearing the mist off the sea and the land.

It was going to be a beautiful day, he hoped.

He wouldn't know for sure until he got back to Honfleur and Tamara.

At the edge of the bluff he stopped, a broad grin spreading across his face.

Serena was doing well.

The *Gypsy* rested at an idle, completely blocking the mouth of the cove.

Two men stood on the deck of the *Marionette*, their arms in the sky. Two of Serena's crew were already hauling a suitcase through the hatch and hoisting it to the *Gypsy*.

Serena herself sat in a lounge chair on the upper deck, beaming, a drink in one hand, a cigarette in the other. She looked up, saw Carter, waved, and shouted:

"I hate to, darling, but I guess I'll turn this stuff in! It's a good thing I don't hang around with you too much . . . you'd make an honest woman out of me!"

EIGHTEEN

Carter felt drained, wasted. He took a long belt of the scotch in his hand and looked out over the lights of Deauville.

The door opened behind him, and he turned. A weary, red-eyed Weatherby rolled into the room. He flopped his bulk into a chair and let the briefcase in his hand drop to the floor.

"God, when you make a mess, you really make a mess, N3."

"About cleaned up?"

"Yeah. Pity we can't have a mass grave. I need a drink."

Carter moved to the bar. "What about the Madonna?"

"Nothing. We put two more professional divers down in the harbor. Zilch."

Carter sighed as he passed a glass to Weatherby. "Tamara said the neck of the oar cover when it was brought up was strung tight. I don't think the Madonna was ever in it. Marta Penn did something else with it."

"Yeah, but what? We've sealed off every house, every hotel room, every apartment connected with this mess. We've picked up everybody even remotely connected, including poor Sedji Cadiz. Nothing."

"Did you find anything down the hall in Marta Penn's suite?"

Weatherby shook his head, emptied his glass, and held it

187

...or a refill. "We even went back over the *Gypsy*, just in
...se Serena was pulling a fast one on you and keeping it out
...om the rest of the loot. Nothing."

Carter grinned broadly. "I didn't think there would be.
Serena is enjoying her day in the sun on the right side of the
law."

"I know," Weatherby groaned. "She's also demanding
we make up the difference between what the insurance pays
and a million."

"A deal is a deal," Carter shrugged. "Even though we
haven't got the Madonna, we know the other side doesn't
have it either."

A young agent put his head inside the door. "Sir?"

"Yeah," Weatherby replied.

"We have the Penn woman's things. You said Mr. Carter
might want to go through them."

Weatherby looked at Carter, who shrugged.

"Put them there by the door."

A suitcase and a cardboard box were deposited, and the
man withdrew.

Carter poured another pair of drinks, and the two men fell
silent. After several minutes, Weatherby spoke.

"Where is she?"

"Other room, dressing."

"I'm here . . . ready."

Carter looked up and smiled. She looked like a fresh-
scrubbed teen-ager again, vulnerable, innocent, yet strangely
exciting.

In a way, he would be sorry to see her go. The weeks of
debriefing in Washington would be hell. And the months of
easing into a new life and a new identity wouldn't be much
better.

Weatherby heaved himself from the chair and picked up
his briefcase. "We'll drive down to Paris tonight. Your plane
leaves at one o'clock tomorrow afternoon."

Carter saw Tamara's eyes dart toward him. He could read
them.

They said: *You drive me to Paris, Nick . . . one la* *night* . . . .

He was tempted, sorely tempted. But he knew it was impossible. There was probably no chance that he could still uncover the Madonna, but he had to try.

Weatherby hoisted Marta Penn's bag with his free hand. "You don't need to go through this stuff, do you?"

"No," Carter replied, "I see no reason for it."

Weatherby kicked the cardboard box. "The hotel staff can toss this bread."

"What?" Carter said.

"Bread, five loaves of bread. Somebody delivered it to the hotel this morning."

Carter exchanged one quick look with Tamara, and as one they dived for the box.

Everything was quiet for a while, then the woman left. She went over there, to that bakery behind the restaurant. She's still there . . . .

Tamara found it in the third loaf. She cracked the hard-crusted bread open, and it just fell into her lap.

"Well, I'll be damned," Weatherby said.

"Listen, old man, you look beat," Carter said. "Why don't I drive the lady to Paris?"

"Suits me."

Carter tossed him the Madonna and gathered Tamara under his arm.

"Guess what?" he whispered, guiding her from the room.

"What?"

"We're going to treat ourselves."

"We are?" she asked, laughing. "To what?"

"A night at the Ritz."

DON'T MISS THE NEXT NEW
NICK CARTER SPY THRILLER

WHITE DEATH

Carter breathed deeply, waiting.

The helicopter moved on, doing thoroughly once what the Soviet jet had done quickly three times.

Carter allowed himself a small smile of triumph, then he tested his body for bruises and broken bones. He was intact, but very tired. He would make camp as soon as he could find a good sheltered spot.

Once more he slogged up the slope, his remarkable stamina and strength surging new power back into his exhausted body.

At the top again where the mountains spread around him in a rocky panorama, he skied on, dipping in and out of canyons, following the skimobile's trail.

Time passed, the Antarctic sun making little progress. Carter watched for a good campsite.

At last he rounded a bend in layered shadows where ɔoulders and snowslides covered a flat apron of land.

The snow gave a good level spot, not large, but large enough. The boulders offered good shelter. Some as large as rooms, they'd spilled one on top of the other until a roof formed over part of the flat area.

Carter dropped his backpack beneath the roof.

He'd pitch the tent here, a shelter against another storm. He'd be protected from helicopter surveillance by the boulders above.

Then he saw the shadow move.

Amid the sounds of dropping snow and distant avalanches, he heard the slick noise of a ski sliding.

It was across from him, someone entering the flat area from the other side.

Quickly he pulled on his backpack, took off his mitten, and flipped his stiletto into his hand. In Antarctica, only a madman shot a gun. The noise would cause avalanches and destruction for miles around.

He skied swiftly back out the way he'd come. He was careful to stay in the same tracks.

When he was out of sight of the flat area, he looked over his shoulder and saw his single ski trail. He heard the sounds of the other skier, heard the pause as the skier discovered Carter's trail, then the rapidity of strokes as he pursued Carter.

Carter swung his arms and leaped off the trail, landing on his back in the soft snow.

With his mitten and arm he brushed the snowbank smooth again as he backed off behind an enormous boulder.

With luck, the pursuer would see only the ski trail continuing on with the skimobile tracks.

Carter skied quietly around the boulder to where he could watch the newcomer's pursuit.

The slip-slide of the oncoming skis were muffled sounds in the Antarctic stillness, the noises absorbed by the vast snow.

First Carter saw the peaked blue fiberfill hat that was

fastened beneath the chin, then the thick blue parka an.
trousers. The skis were Russian.

The man was small, agile, his face bent low as he studied
Carter's trail.

As he came in sight of the place where Carter had jumped
off, he slowed. He raised his face to scan ahead.

Carter smiled.

It was Blenkochev's comrade, the man with the yellow
Mazda.

The expression on the small-featured face was one of
puzzlement. Something wasn't right, the expression said, but
he wasn't sure exactly what. He skied ahead slowly.

Swiftly Carter returned around the boulder to follow.

The knife glinted in the sun.

The assistant's knife was waiting for Carter where he'd
jumped off the trail. It was now Blenkochev's pal's turn to
smile. He'd figured out Carter's trick in leaving the trail.
He'd doubled back to meet him.

"You shouldn't be here," the Russian agent said softly,
the knife pointed at Carter's chin. He spoke in English.

"Why not?" Carter answered in Russian, showing his
stiletto.

The stiletto was a diversion.

He threw the other hand up and knocked the Russian's
knife flying.

The Russian's toe clips were already released. His boots
free, he kicked.

"Because this is none of your business!" he said.

Carter ducked.

The Russian changed targets. His foot unerringly caught
the stiletto in Carter's hand, sending Hugo flying overhead.

Quickly Carter unsnapped his skis from his feet.

The knife and stiletto were nowhere in sight.

The two agents thrashed through the snow. Circled. Their
boots sank six inches into the soft powder.

Again the Russian's foot lashed out.

Carter caught it.

The Russian twisted.

Carter yanked.

Caught by the snow, the two fell forward.

Wrestled.

Suddenly Carter veered back, his eyes wide.

Breasts. The Russian had breasts. A woman. Why the walk was different. Why the tam-o'-shanter was pulled low to the ears.

The woman swung a fist.

Carter spun to the side.

He reached back, unsnapped the chin strap, and whipped up the woman's blue peaked cap.

Long flaxen hair cascaded to the shoulders of the blue parka. The hair was like strands of silk, flying free in the icy Antarctic air. The small-featured face came into perspective. A too-small man turned into a beautifully proportioned woman with full lips, straight nose, and wide eyes bright under the cold sun. She was the blonde in the airport photograph Mike had shown him. The beautiful blonde.

"I'll be damned," Carter murmured.

"Took you long enough," she said, slugging him in the chin. "It works every time."

Taken by surprise, reeling from the blow, Carter slugged back.

She went limp.

He caught her before she hit the ground. He hadn't intended to knock her out.

She was light. Her head fell back, the pale blond hair drifting long to the snow.

—From *WHITE DEATH*
A New Nick Carter Spy Thriller
From Charter in August 1985